THE 12 GIFTS OF Christmas

LENA NELSON DOOLEY

THE 12 GIFTS OF Christmas

WHITAKER
HOUSE

THE 12 GIFTS OF CHRISTMAS

www.lenanelsondooley.com
http://lenanelsondooley.blogspot.com
http://www.blogtalkradio.com/search/along-came-a-writer
www.instagram.com/lenanelsondooley

ISBN: 978-1-64123-148-0
eBook ISBN: 978-1-64123-149-7
Printed in the United States of America
© 2018 by Lena Nelson Dooley

Whitaker House
1030 Hunt Valley Circle
New Kensington, PA 15068
www.whitakerhouse.com

Library of Congress Cataloging-in-Publication Data (Pending)

1 2 3 4 5 6 7 8 9 10 11 ⨃ 26 25 24 23 22 21 20 19 18

DEDICATION

*T*his book is dedicated to my very best friend, Rita Booth. My husband, James, and I met Rita and David Booth about thirty years ago. They were missionaries to Mexico, and God tied all four of our heartstrings together in a knot that couldn't be untied. David has gone on to meet Jesus before the rest of us, and we miss his quick wit and his enormous heart for people. Rita has been closer than a sister to me. We laugh together, we cry together, and we pray for each other and our families. She's my rock. I love you, Rita, higher than the Texas sky.

The missionary story in this book is based on Rita and David's romance.

And every book I write is dedicated to the man who captured my heart fifty-four years ago. The question Malcolm asks Alanza on their first date, James asked me on our second or third. We were married three months and three days after we met on a blind date. He's the better half of me. I pray God allows us to have many, many more years together.

1

Wednesday – Fourteen Days Before Christmas

Malcolm MacGregor glanced around the dining room of Cantalamessa's Gourmet Pizzas and More on Highway 10 in Euless, Texas. Each time he'd eaten here, he'd chosen to sit at an out-of-the-way table, separated from most other patrons. With a major project he had nearing completion, he often worked through the lunch hour, even when he went out to eat. This was the perfect place to do it, and the same table where he'd sat before was free. He took a seat, opened his briefcase, and pulled out his laptop. Soon, he was deep into his work.

It was the third time he'd come here since a coworker told him about this place a couple weeks ago. He'd never been fond of the typical American pizza, with its cheap cheese, watery sauce, and way too many greasy spiced meats. But the pizzas here were works of culinary art. Not too doughy and plenty of healthy options. He'd tried a couple different kinds and each was delicious.

"Hey, welcome back." It was the same cheerful waiter who had served him before. He handed a menu to Malcolm. "What would you like to drink?"

"Thanks. Dr Pepper, please."

"Should I call that your usual?"

Malcolm laughed. "Sure. Thanks for remembering."

"I'll be right back with it, ready to take your order."

Malcolm watched him walk away, then turned to the all-important file on his screen. In one worksheet, the figures weren't adding up. He had to find the discrepancy, so he could move forward.

Malcolm's employer provided specialized equipment for hospitals and medical centers throughout the United States. They recently launched a new division with a charitable outreach arm. Malcolm was keenly aware of its importance—not for himself, but for the patients it would serve. His employer was setting up mobile medical clinics in rural areas, walking the fine line between making enough profit to ensure they stayed open and keeping fees low enough that patients could afford them, even if they had a high-deductible health insurance plan, or no coverage at all. He was also putting together grant proposals to help those with the greatest needs.

Not much time passed before the waiter returned with the soft drink. Malcolm looked up from his laptop.

"What can I get you today? I know you like Dr Pepper, but I think you've ordered different pizzas each time you were here."

Malcolm smiled and glanced at the waiter's nametag. Ignazio. He appreciated waiters who remembered customers and their preferences. "I'd like to go off-menu today and get a pizza with spinach, artichoke hearts, mushrooms, and basil."

Ignazio made notes on his pad. "That sounds good. Maybe we should put this on the menu. Would you like anything else on it? Maybe extra mozzarella?"

"Sure."

As the young man headed toward the kitchen, Malcolm went back to his work. He had to make sure the figures were correct. He started going through the columns with a fine-tooth comb. When the error finally jumped out at him, he wanted to shout, "Yay!" *Probably not the place to do that.* There were quite a few patrons here, even though he waited until after 1 p.m., trying to miss the lunch crowd. Cantalamessa's was probably packed from noon to 1 p.m., like many restaurants. Even when he arrived past the regular lunch hour, there was always a nice-sized crowd here.

"Here you are." Ignazio set the enticing concoction in front of him.

"Thank you. This smells delicious."

"Careful, the pan is hot."

"That's what makes it so good. Coming straight from the oven to the table."

As Ignazio walked away, Malcolm closed his eyes and said a silent prayer of thanks.

When he raised his head, he noticed the beautiful young woman who usually ran the cash register. Alanza, her nametag said. He couldn't be the only one who noticed how gorgeous she was. But Malcolm always looked beneath a woman's surface beauty. Alanza's eyes seemed to be windows to her heart. At first, he was fascinated by the unusual green in her irises. They were the color of budding tree leaves in early spring.

His best friend, Eric Summerfield, had dated a lot of different girls and women—in high school, college, graduate school, and even now. Dating was just a thing for him. He never seemed to be serious about anyone. Malcolm wondered if Eric would ever settle down with just one woman. He knew if Eric ever saw Alanza, all he would see was her lovely figure. Not her inner self.

She was tall, probably near six feet. She seemed confident, but in a gentle, easy way. Happiness and joy flowed around her, drawing other people to her. He'd watched her interact with customers in a way that let him know she really cared about people. He'd even seen her helping the busboys and waiters.

Malcolm forced his attention back to his files while he savored his pizza. Ignazio came and went, bringing him refills of Dr Pepper when his glass was empty. When all of his work was finally in order, Malcolm happily clicked the save button. The project was finished. He closed his computer and slipped it into his briefcase.

When he glanced up, Malcolm's gaze was drawn to Alanza. He hadn't dated a lot because he had asked God to direct him to the woman He'd prepared to be his wife. Ever since he first laid eyes on Alanza, he wondered if she could be the one.

An older man came out of the kitchen area and hugged her.

"Poppa! You're back." She threw her arms around his neck.

Malcolm noticed some similarities between them. Was she the owner's daughter? If so, he needed to pay more attention to them. If she *was* the woman God had for him, Malcolm would be speaking to her father one day—hopefully soon—to ask for her hand in marriage. Malcolm wouldn't even date a woman without her father's permission. His family was very traditional.

For the rest of his meal, he watched Alanza and her father's every move. The older man made the rounds of the restaurant, stopping and leisurely talking to the customers as if they were old friends. No wonder this restaurant had such a loyal clientele.

Malcolm didn't wait for Alanza's father to reach him. He wanted to get back to the office and felt he'd wasted enough time already. *Not wasted.* Watching the lovely Alanza sped up his heartbeat more than his workouts did. He'd never experienced that feeling before.

When he went to the register, Alanza was talking to another worker. Malcolm leaned against the counter beside the cash register and waited. The man gave Alanza a slight nod and left for the kitchen.

She quickly turned toward Malcolm. When their eyes met, everything around them seemed to fade away. Alanza looked as surprised as he felt. For a moment or two, he couldn't remember why he was there. Finally, he took a deep breath, and the connection was broken. He pulled a credit card from his wallet and slid it across the counter toward her, along with his bill.

"Was everything all right…" She lifted his card and glanced at his name. "…Mr. MacGregor? You've been in here a couple of times recently, I think. I guess you liked it, uh…" An attractive blush tinted her cheeks and her green eyes sparkled like a forest after rainfall.

"Call me Malcolm. Yes. I love your pizzas. Maybe I'll try some pasta next time."

She handed him a receipt to sign.

When he finished, he glanced up at her and caught her eyes roaming over his face and upper body. The blush deepened and seeped to her hairline. She was even more beautiful up close.

"Now that you know my name, may I ask your name?"

Her eyes widened. The pulse at the base of her neck started beating double-time. "Alanza Cantalamessa." Her answer was so soft, he almost missed it.

"So, you're the owner's daughter?" He raised an eyebrow.

She gave an expansive gesture taking in almost all of the workers. "Many people who work here are members of my extended family. Ignazio is my cousin. My parents own Cantalamessa's."

Malcolm smiled and pushed his wallet into the hip pocket of his suit pants. "I'm really glad a friend told me about this place." He didn't take his eyes off her face while he made a declaration. "And I'll be back soon."

Did her smile grow even wider? Sure looked that way.

On the trip to the office, his Beemer was almost on autopilot. His thoughts kept returning to Cantalamessa's and the beautiful Alanza.

ALANZA'S GAZE FOLLOWED Malcolm MacGregor as he strode to the front door. Before he opened it, he glanced back at her one more time and gave her a broad smile. *Holy cow, he's so handsome! Why is my heart almost jumping out of my chest?*

All afternoon, she kept thinking about him. He was tall, with the thick, wavy auburn hair and eyes the color of a Texas summer sky. He had to be a businessman, with his sharp-looking suits and laptop. Why did he come to the restaurant alone? Most businessmen came in groups, or at least with a lunch date or a friend.

She didn't see a ring on his left hand. And there wasn't a white line where one would be if he'd worn a wedding ring out in the sun but had taken it off. Could he possibly be single? Her heart beat faster and she took a deep breath to try to calm down.

What difference would it make anyway? Poppa always said he hoped she'd marry a good, Christian Italian man. Of course, Poppa didn't marry a good, Christian Italian. Mamma was a strong Christian, but they met in Brazil when he visited Buenos Aires for spring break during his senior year at college. He laughingly called her his "Girl from Ipanema." He thought of that song when he first saw her. She was almost six feet tall and had a glorious tan from spending time at the beach.

Alanza was like that, too. She never got sunburned. Her skin just darkened.

Mamma was only nineteen when she stole Poppa's heart. Alanza had heard the stories many times. How Mamma had been heartbroken when Poppa returned to the United States. How she prayed he'd return to her, even though they'd spent less than a week together. How surprised she was when only a month later, she's watched him walk along the beach at sunset... right toward her. Grandpapa would never let Mamma go to America with a man he hardly knew. So Poppa had to stay until Grandpapa would let her go. They were both stubborn men... but Grandpapa quickly realized just how much Mamma and Poppa loved each other. And the two men made sure the families got together at least once a year—either in Brazil or in the U.S.

And here Alanza was, three years out of college, and she'd never had the heart-stopping kind of experience her parents talked about. *Until now.*

Whatever happened when she saw and talked to Malcolm MacGregor was strong. She had experienced all kinds of visceral reactions. Breathlessness. Rapid heartbeat. Hummingbirds flitting around her insides, their wings beating right in time with her racing pulse.

Poppa had always talked about her and her siblings marrying other Italians. He would probably have a cow if he knew what she was thinking. With a name like MacGregor, he had to be Scottish. There were lots of miles between Scotland and Italy.

"Alanza."

She jumped.

Her mother's voice penetrated her tumultuous thoughts. "A line is forming. Do you need help?"

"No, ma'am."

Giving herself a mental shake, she turned back toward the cash register. Four regular customers stood ready to pay their bills.

"How was everything today, ladies?"

2

Thursday – Thirteen Days Before Christmas

After spending an almost sleepless night communicating with God, Malcolm dragged himself out of bed. He wolfed down a bagel with strawberry cream cheese, barely tasting it, and gulped some strong black coffee. He was sluggish when he shaved and got dressed, too. How would he ever make it through the day?

He needed more caffeine. He stopped for an espresso on the way to work. Later, he'd have to reload. He probably wouldn't sleep any better tonight, but tomorrow started the weekend, and he could sleep all day Saturday, if he needed to, to catch up on the rest he missed.

As soon as Malcolm got to the office and set down the coffee, his assistant put through a call from Frank Talbot, the company president.

"Hello, sir." Malcolm dropped into his leather chair, then took another sip of coffee.

"I've been looking over this business plan you sent me late yesterday."

Malcolm was sure he couldn't remember all of the details in the plan, he was so tired. And it seemed like a lot had happened since he had submitted it. His mind and heart had been heavily invested in seeking an answer from the Lord last night. He hoped he wouldn't need to explain something before he was able to read over the paperwork again.

"I'd like to see you in my office, Malcolm. Right now."

Great. Maybe he should take his laptop with him, so he could see what his boss was looking at. He grabbed it and headed up to the executive suite floor.

Talbot was waiting by the elevator when the doors slid open. Malcolm glanced at his face. *Happy or angry? Happy. That's good.*

"Come on in." The boss led the way into his office, then shut the door behind them. *Must be important, since he closed the door. Something he doesn't want anyone else to hear.*

Malcolm loved the view from this height. Floor-to-ceiling windows let in lots of sunlight, even in the wintertime. Since this was the largest office on the floor, taking up half of the footage, he could see a panorama of downtown Fort Worth and the surrounding area. Traffic was heavy through the Mix Master. Malcolm always tried to get to work early to miss most of it.

When Talbot moved to the large leather chair behind his desk, Malcolm dropped into one of the two chairs across from him. "How can I help you, sir? Do you need me to explain anything?"

Talbot gave a belly laugh, sounding almost like a mall Santa. "No, Malcolm, you do such excellent work, it's easy to understand. And I'm about to help *you*."

Malcolm had no idea what the boss was talking about. He didn't need any help...except to stay awake.

"The executive board met in special session last night. We're moving on this project—quickly." Talbot's smile was so wide, Malcolm could have counted his teeth.

Okay, great. But what's this have to do with me? Malcolm rubbed his hands down the rosewood arms of his chair. The caffeine was starting to make him feel jumpy. This day couldn't end soon enough—and it was still early morning.

"We're proud of all you've done to bring about this agreement. We've already been in touch with the people in Brisbane. We'll send a team down there by late January. And you'll head up the team." Talbot's satisfied smile looked like he was the cat that ate the canary, as his *Faither* often said.

Wait a minute. What?

"Yes, you heard me right. You'll head up the team." Talbot had never looked this happy around Malcolm. It almost made him nervous. "You'll be going as the Vice President of Global Resources."

Talbot then started talking about setting up the new office in Australia, timetables, getting around in Brisbane, how Malcolm's work would be covered while he was away, renting an apartment, Down Under cuisine... He was talking faster than Malcolm could keep up with. He needed more caffeine to kick in—right now. "A promotion to Vice President? And a transfer to Australia? Did I hear you right?"

"It's a lot to take in, I know. But we've been watching you and planning to promote you if you came through with this project. And you did. Just the way we thought you would."

Talbot stood and came around the desk to lean against it near where Malcolm sat.

"I'll be moving to Australia? This is kind of sudden. I'm not sure—"

"Maybe I phrased that wrong. You won't be moving there per se. It's a six-month assignment to get the Australian office up and running. Then you'll return here to start working on the next expansion phase."

Malcolm rose from his chair and held out his hand. "Thank you, sir, for believing in me."

After they shook hands, his boss furrowed his brows as he looked into Malcolm's face. "You've been working hard on this. Why don't you take the rest of the day off? We'll see you back on Monday."

Thank You, Jesus!

Malcolm almost shouted and gave a fist pump in the elevator. But with its walls of glass, that would never do. He restrained himself.

He grabbed the briefcase from his office and headed out the door. "I'll be off the rest of the day, Christine. See you on Monday."

His assistant stared at him as if he'd grown another head. He never took off early like that. He stopped and turned back to pop back in briefly. "You can take the rest of the day off, too… with pay."

He could feel her eyes following him until he entered the elevator. He was sure there would be lots of work for her on Monday. She could use a break, too.

As Malcolm walked across the third level of the parking garage, his mind whirled in several directions. *I'm going to Australia for six months.* He stopped walking. That meant he wouldn't see Alanza for six months. After all the time he spent with God last night, he was sure of one thing. She was God's choice for his wife. Did he want to wait that long to get to know her better and share what God had told him? *Of course not!*

He had to do something. He'd have to talk to her father and convince him this was God's plan. He'd have to convince Alanza. Even his own father probably wouldn't understand right away. But he wasn't going to go to another continent without his wife. This might be a little tricky, but he would try to listen closely to God as he moved through all the minefields. And he expected plenty of them.

After he got into his car, he sat there thinking. A plan formed in his mind. He knew it came from God. He couldn't have come up with anything like this in a million years.

Before he started the engine, he called his youngest sister.

"Bella, you know that hair thingy you made with the MacGregor tartan ribbon I ordered for you?" He hoped he wasn't making a mistake calling her.

"Of course I do. It's my favorite claw clip. Thanks again, bro."

"Did you use all the ribbon?"

"I didn't even use half of it. Why?"

"I want you to make one for me. I'll order you more ribbon to replace what you use." There. He'd blurted it as fast as he could.

"When do you want it?" He could hear the curiosity in Arabella's voice.

"By tomorrow, if possible." *What will she say to that? I hope she'll just agree without asking too many questions!*

"Mal, I know you wouldn't wear this, so you must want it for a woman. When you ordered this spool of ribbon from Scotland for my birthday, I never dreamed you'd ask me to create another hair clip with it. Who's it for?"

He should have prepared himself for this. Despite all that was on his mind, he should have realized his crafty sister wouldn't make the gift without asking who it was for. But he didn't have the time or the inclination to tell anyone yet. "You don't know her."

What else can I say? She's the woman of my dreams? I plan to marry her before leaving for Australia for six months? No one knew about any of this, the woman or Australia. He couldn't tell anyone until after he made the first overture to Alanza. Just the thought of her filled his heart and head. Her dancing green eyes and black cloud of hair framing her exquisite face. How breathless he felt when their eyes met. He could feel the heat creep up his throat and into his cheeks even now.

"That's no answer. Who is this woman?"

"Sis, that's all I can tell you right now. Can you make it for me…by tomorrow? Please?"

"Oh, all right." She sighed.

He heard the reluctance in Arabella's voice. He'd have to do something special for her. And she'd be the first person in his family he would tell about Alanza when he was ready to let them know what was going on.

Malcolm was surprised when his sister called him early in the afternoon. He hadn't expected her to finish until tomorrow. He headed over to the house to pick it up when he knew his grandmother would be napping. He figured he'd have to face another inquisition from Bella. Maybe that was why she finished so quickly.

"Come in, Mal." They went into her bedroom.

She picked up an almost finished hair clip.

"When I asked you who this is for, you didn't answer me— as if it doesn't make any difference? But it does. Who is this woman?" Bella pressed her lips into a tight line then added a drop of hot melt glue at each end of the ribbon, anchoring it to the black clip.

Malcolm turned away. What could he say without having to explain himself? "Bel, I have to get back to work. What do I owe you?"

"The information about who this is for." His sister stood and held the clip behind her back. "You won't get it till you tell me." With her head thrown back and her chin raised in the air, she looked so much like their dearly departed *Mither*. Her bright red curls formed curlicues that bounced around her head.

For a moment, he couldn't force out a single word. If this was his brother instead of his youngest sister, Malcolm would have forced her to hand over the hair ornament. He glanced around her bedroom. On top of her dresser, her purse lay open, her hot pink cell phone peeking out of the top.

He reached over and grabbed the phone. "I don't have time for this. I have a lot I need to get done today. I'll just keep this until you're ready to give me the clip."

She lowered her head and brought the hand holding the hair clip out from behind her back. Sighed. "I know you wouldn't have me make this if there wasn't a special woman involved, Mal. After all, the ribbon is our tartan design. You don't give a tartan gift to just anyone. Only if you're engaged or something. So why haven't we heard about her?" She held out the ribbon clip in one hand and opened the other to receive her phone.

He dropped the phone into her empty hand and quickly lifted the hair clip from the other. "I can't tell you yet. There is a woman... and she is special to me... but... I'll tell you about her when it's time."

Malcolm didn't want to lie to Bella. Before she could get out another question, he left her room and hurried down the stairs, taking two steps at a time. He was out the door and into his BMW before she could catch him. She waved to him as he peeled out of the driveway.

He prayed she wouldn't go blabbing anything to the rest of the family. With more time, and if he hadn't been so tired, he could have handled the matter with more finesse.

SINCE HE WORKED in Fort Worth and his apartment was in a gated community in East Euless, he always beat Eric home. His roommate had to drive through all the rush hour traffic from the eastern side of North Dallas.

Malcolm smiled to himself as he parked the car. Eric's Mustang was nowhere to be seen. Malcolm grabbed his suit jacket and briefcase and headed inside.

Even though it was December, it felt more like early summer. The weather had been crazy this year. Out-of-season temperatures. Spotty, brief rainfalls, leaving everything in near-drought conditions. And the weather forecasters said there could be snow by the middle of next week.

He left his briefcase on the table, then pulled out the hair clip and placed it on top so it wouldn't get crushed. After changing into jeans and a sweater *Mither* had knitted for him when he went to Texas A&M, he grabbed the mail and started separating it into three stacks: his mail, Eric's mail, and junk mail. Typical for December, the junk mail pile was the tallest. Malcolm dumped it into the kitchen trash can.

When Eric entered the apartment, the first thing he saw was the hair clip.

"What's this? Have you been entertaining some girl before I got home?" Eric chuckled.

"I wish."

Eric stared at him for a moment. "Okay, Mal, what's up?"

"Nothing." Malcolm picked up the clip with the loopy bow, slowly and carefully turning it over and over. *Bella really is so clever.*

"Wait a minute," Eric demanded. "Whose is that?"

"It's just a gift for someone." Malcolm glanced down at the frilly hair clip.

"That's your tartan," Eric said, "and you Scottish men don't give a girl something with your tartan on it unless you're serious about her." He dragged a chair away from the kitchen table and turned it around to straddle it. "What gives?"

Malcolm was getting tired of all this subterfuge. And it had been too long since he'd had any caffeine. He heaved a deep sigh. "I was going to tell you later, but here goes. I have to go to Australia for six months. Don't worry, I'll still pay my half of the rent. And I want to get married before I go."

Eric gave his head a quick shake. He looked as if he'd been hit by a two-by-four. "Are you nuts? You're not even dating anyone! Who are you talking about—someone you met online? And what do you mean, going to Australia?"

Malcolm sighed and went to the fridge to get a cold Dr Pepper. He popped the tab off the can and guzzled about half of it. "Want a soda?"

His roommate nodded. Malcolm grabbed a Coke and handed it to Eric.

Turning and leaning against the edge of the cabinet, Malcolm crossed his arms. *Where should I start?* "Australia was the biggest surprise of my life, man. My boss liked the presentation I sent him just before I left work yesterday. He actually called a board meeting last night and they all liked my proposal. So they contacted the people in Australia. I'll be going there for six months to get a satellite office off the ground. And I've been promoted." He smiled. "You're looking at the Vice President of Global Resources."

Eric jumped up and gave him a fist bump. "Way to go, bro!"

"Yeah..." Malcolm stared off into the distance, thinking about Alanza. His heart started thumping. *Is she working tomorrow? Will she like the hair clip? And how am I ever going to approach her father?*

"Earth to Malcolm." Eric's words broke into his thoughts.

He glanced over at his roommate, who had dropped down onto the sofa. *When did he move over there?*

"Okay." Eric gave him a funny smile. "I can see that something has you off-track. And I think I know what it is. I've seen that same expression on other guys' faces when they go loopy over a girl. Never thought it'd happen to you. So who is this hottie?"

Malcolm frowned. He wasn't sure he wanted his best friend to call Alanza a *hottie*.

"Remember a couple of weeks ago I told you about Cantalamessa's Gourmet Pizzas and More over on Highway 10?"

"Yeah, so?" Eric stared intently at him.

"Well, I've gone there for lunch a few times."

Eric leaned his arms along the back of the sofa and stared at Malcolm. "Okay, so?"

"Well... There's a woman who works as a cashier. Her parents own the place. I go to work while I eat and, uh... watch her."

"Man, isn't that stalking?" Eric looked worried. "You could get into real trouble for that."

"No, no, nothing like that. We've only talked while I paid... and only about the payment." This was beginning to sound crazy.

How could he make his friend understand? "Look, I've wanted to get to know her, but there hasn't been a good opportunity."

"So what's different now?" Eric stood and headed toward the fridge.

"With my promotion, I'll have to be in Australia for at least six months." He couldn't look at his best friend while he was telling this story. He stared out the patio door. "I want to take her with me as my wife."

"Your wife?" Eric's voice almost became a screech. "Does insanity run in your family or what?"

3

Friday – Twelve Days Before Christmas

Malcolm pulled into the empty parking lot of Cantalamessa's at nine Friday morning. When he'd called and asked to speak to Mr. Cantalamessa, then told him he would like to stop by and would appreciate a few minutes of his time, the man hadn't asked what he wanted. Just told him to come at nine before the restaurant opened. The front door was unlocked, so Malcolm stepped inside. Alessandro Cantalamessa was working on some papers, sitting at the table where Malcolm usually sat. Malcolm headed toward him.

"Mr. Cantalamessa." He sat in the chair across from Alanza's father, who greeted him with a handshake.

"Would you like coffee or Dr Pepper?"

"Dr Pepper is fine, sir, thank you."

Alessandro gestured to someone behind the counter, and Ignazio soon arrived with the soda and a steaming cup of coffee.

Malcolm smiled at him. "Thank you, Ignazio."

With a nod, the waiter went to the front door and locked it, then returned to his task behind the counter.

Alessandro laid his pen on the table. "What can I do for you, Malcolm?" He got right to the point.

Malcolm appreciated his directness and he didn't want to take up too much of his time. He'd rehearsed what he would say... but somehow, the words escaped him now that they were face-to-face.

"Uh... I know you don't know much about me." He hoped his face wasn't as red as it felt.

"I know enough." Alessandro gave him a nod. "Go ahead."

"I've noticed Alanza..."

"As do a lot of men." Now, his smile wasn't quite as warm.

Maybe a different tack would work better. "I'm a Christian, so I don't date frivolously. I have to tell you, sir, Alanza has touched a place in my heart."

The smile disappeared. Things weren't looking good. But at least he wasn't frowning.

"I'd like your permission to get to know her better... start dating... with marriage in mind." Malcolm gulped. He never dreamed how hard this would be. *Why did I mention marriage so soon?*

He knew what God told him Thursday night, but how could he possibly tell her father what He said? Even when he roiled the words over in his own mind, they sounded like the kind of line a man with bad intentions might use. But usually with the young woman herself, not her father.

"Has my daughter indicated she's interested in dating you?"

Malcolm hadn't expected that question. *What can I say? Yes? No? I'm not sure?* "Actually, sir, we haven't spoken much except when I've paid for my meals. I didn't want to approach her to ask her out until I had your permission."

"Not many young men do that these days." Alessandro's smile returned. "I respect you for that."

"Thank you, sir." *Were things looking up?* What direction should he take the conversation now?

"Ignazio." Alanza's father motioned to his nephew, who hurried over again.

"Do you need refills?"

"No. Would you please tell Alanza I want to see her?"

"Of course." The waiter nodded then headed toward the kitchen's swinging doors.

"So do you live close by?" Alessandro Cantalamessa looked Malcolm square in the eyes.

Malcolm guessed they were going to have a casual conversation until she got to the table. "Yes, sir, in an apartment in Euless. But I work in Fort Worth."

"I've seen you working while you have lunch here. Usually, businessmen don't come alone." His countenance relaxed a little. "What do you do?"

"Well, I recently received a promotion. I'm a vice president at—"

"Poppa, what do you need?" Alanza's melodious voice was a welcome interruption.

No telling what her father would ask next. Malcolm stood, and so did Alanza's father.

"I want to ask you a question." Alessandro gave his daughter an indulgent smile. His love for her lit up the area.

"Sure, Poppa."

Malcolm could tell she was wondering what was going on. He was afraid her father was going to ask if she wanted to date him. He really didn't want her to answer that question with him standing right beside her. He wanted an honest answer, not one she felt forced to make because she didn't want to embarrass him. He flashed her a quick smile, hoping it would help her relax.

"You've met Mr. MacGregor, haven't you?"

"Yes, I've worked the cash register when he's paid for his food." She smiled at Malcolm. "Hello, Mr. MacGregor. Good to see you again. But we don't open for another half an hour."

Her father sat down again. "Let's all sit down," he said. Alanza sat down beside him.

"MacGregor here came to ask me if he could date you."

Her eyes widened, but she didn't look upset. That was a good sign.

"Oh, he did, did he?"

"I did not want to give him my answer until I knew if you in fact wanted to date him."

Now a blush crept up her cheeks, making her even more beautiful. And her green eyes sparkled. He'd never noticed the tiny golden flecks in her irises before. He tried to keep his face neutral, but it was hard when he wished he had the right to pull her into his arms right then and there.

Her smile widened. "Sure. I'd like that."

He hoped she didn't feel pressured. "How about tonight?" he asked. "Would you like to go out to dinner?"

Alessandro clapped his hands softly a couple of times. "Bravo. Now, that's settled. Do you need anything else, Malcolm?"

He pulled his attention from Alanza toward her father. "No, sir. Thank you."

They shook hands. "Now, please excuse me, I must finish this." And Alessandro returned to his paperwork.

The bright smile Alanza flashed him went straight to his heart. *I praise and thank You, Lord, for this beautiful woman You have created for me.*

"What time?"

What time? When does she get off work? As soon as possible would be good. Calm down and think straight!

"What time would work for you, Alanza?"

"How about seven?"

"Fine. Where do you live? I'll come pick you up there."

After Alanza gave him the address, he said his goodbyes, then went out to his car, unable to stop smiling. *It's going to happen!*

ALANZA HAD A hard time keeping her mind on work. Malcolm MacGregor asked Poppa if he could date her! Wow. She didn't think he realized how often she gazed over at him while he was in the restaurant. It had become a habit for her to glance at the door every time it opened between one and two p.m. Even though she knew she'd see him tonight and he had no reason to come back in for lunch, she still looked up every single time the door opened. She hoped no one noticed… especially not Poppa.

When it was almost five, her father stopped by the cash register. "Alanza, you can go home and get ready for your date tonight."

"But, Poppa, the evening rush will start soon. I could stay at least an hour longer."

He gave her one of his special smiles. "No, I want you to have plenty of time to get ready."

That's all it took. She whipped off her apron and headed to the employee break room to get her things out of her locker. In less than ten minutes, she drove toward her apartment, her heart singing.

While getting ready, she thought about all of the things she liked about Malcolm MacGregor. She loved him being so much taller than she was. At five-foot-eleven, not many men were. She could even wear high heels and not be as tall as he was. He had to be at least six-foot-three—maybe more. He looked strong, but not too buff. Not like those crazy guys who worked out so much that they were musclebound. His sky-blue eyes held intelligence, humor, and warmth. She'd never been interested in a guy with red hair before. But his was a rich auburn with just enough waviness that she'd never seen it in disarray. And when he'd leaned on the counter and talked to her while paying his bill, he smelled very masculine and woodsy. It lingered in the air for a few moments after he left the restaurant.

Alanza sang along with the playlist on her smart phone while in the shower and blow drying her hair. When she went to her walk-in closet, she couldn't decide what to wear. Why hadn't she asked Malcolm where they were going? She didn't know whether to dress up or dress down.

It had started to get chilly before she left work and it would get really cold after the sun went down, so she decided to dress in layers. Navy slacks with knee-high black boots. A rich green, long-sleeved blouse with an attached scarf that tied into a bow near her throat. On top of that, her favorite sweater in shades of green and navy. Then she pulled out a long wool coat with a quilted lining.

Alanza glanced at the clock. *He'll be here in fifteen minutes. Will he be early or late? Maybe just on time.*

She hurriedly put on some makeup, finishing with less than five minutes to spare. She went into the living room and dropped the coat and her purse on the sofa. Peeking out between the curtains, she noticed a car that she had never seen in her parking lot before. Someone was sitting in it. Could it be him?

Just as she had that thought, the car door opened, and he stood up and glanced toward her apartment. She moved away from the window and looked at the clock. One minute until seven. She wondered how long he'd been sitting in the car, waiting for seven o'clock. She went to the door just as the doorbell rang.

Alanza took a deep breath and opened the door. Smiled. *Breathe!*

"I like a man who's prompt."

"And I like not having to wait for a woman to finish getting ready." His smile was wide and bright.

Time just seemed to stop as they stood there gazing into each other's eyes, smiling. *Dear Lord, how gorgeous his eyes are!* Finally, she stepped back. "Come in out of the cold."

He wiped his feet on the mat and entered. He had good manners, she was pleased to note.

She closed the door behind him. "I'm ready. I just need to get my coat and purse."

He followed her into the living room. When she lifted her coat, he took it from her.

"Let me help you with this." He held it open for her.

She turned her back to him, so she could slip her arms into the sleeves. Then she turned around again. He surprised her by straightening the collar in the back and buttoning her coat up for her. She watched his fingers, mesmerized, wondering what it would feel like to have him touching her...

"It's gotten much colder than it was this morning. I want to make sure you're snug and warm. Do you need a hat?" His gesture stopped short of touching her hair.

She was taken by his consideration.

"I'm fine."

Once outside, he opened the passenger door of his BMW with his key fob and gave her his hand to help her inside. The engine was running, so the interior was warm. Again, his good manners pleased her.

He climbed into the driver's side and turned the lights on. "You ready?"

"Yes." She nodded. "Where are we going?"

Laying his arms on the top of the steering wheel, he turned toward her. "It's not far. A bistro nearby. The food is good and the tables are arranged so you get some privacy. I'd like us to start getting acquainted right away."

"Me, too," she whispered. He must have heard her because a wide smile spread across his face and his eyes twinkled. Alanza felt as if he was about to drive her to a new world completely foreign to her.

4

*T*his looks like a house. I don't even see a sign." Alanza felt
cozy in the warm BMW as they drove up a long driveway
through a garden with many trees and dormant flowerbeds. She
was sure this would be amazing during spring and summer.

"I think this house was owned by a wealthy family and when
the parents died, their children sold it, so the money could be
divided." Malcolm drove around the side of the house to the
parking lot behind it. "I understand the place needed a lot of
upgrading, so the chef and his wife got a very good deal on it."
He smiled at her.

"Interesting." Malcolm was a fountain of information.

He stopped the car but didn't turn off the engine. "Should
I go back around the house and let you out near the front door?
It's getting pretty windy."

"No." She pulled her coat tighter around her. "I'd rather walk with you than stand inside waiting while you park."

He shut off the engine, got out, and came around to open her door. When she placed her hand in his outstretched one, his warmth ran up her arm and landed somewhere near her stomach.

After he shut the door and locked the car, he placed his arm across her back and held her close as they went up the sidewalk. They were so close there was no space for the wind to get between them. *He's so warm! And feels so strong!*

Alanza had dated in college. Always casually. But this felt different. She wasn't sure she was ready for a serious relationship. Her head cautioned her to be careful, but her heart welcomed his muscular arm around her. She appreciated his thoughtfulness.

They quickly climbed the steps to the screened-in back porch. Perhaps diners sat out here in the warmer months. Before they reached the door, it opened, and a maître d' welcomed them into the warmth of the bistro. "Good evening, Mr. MacGregor. We have your table ready."

Malcolm helped Alanza out of her coat and hung it on a hallway coat tree near the door, then quickly added his coat to hers.

The waiter stood nearby, ready to lead them to their table.

Alanza smiled at the man. "It smells wonderful in here. Malcolm has told me how good the food is."

The waiter smiled back. "I hope you'll enjoy it. Please follow me."

He led them to a secluded table where large potted plants formed a screen around three sides. So that was what Malcolm was talking about. It did give a feeling of privacy.

The waiter pulled out Alanza's chair and pushed it in when she was seated. Then he took the fan-folded napkin off of her plate, shook it out, and placed it on her lap.

"Mr. MacGregor, I know you don't want wine, but will your lady be having some?"

She gave Malcolm a slight shake of her head.

"No, Marcel, Miss Cantalamessa would not like wine either."

Marcel's eyes widened. "Cantalamessa? Like the Italian place out on Highway 10?"

She nodded. "Yes. My family owns it. I'm Alanza."

"I can't believe I didn't recognize you. That's where I go when I want Italian food. It's the best in the Mid-Cities. I know Mr. MacGregor drinks Dr Pepper year-round. Would you like something hot or something cold?"

She gave a slight shiver. "I'll take something hot right now. What do you have?"

"We have three different coffee roasts—dark, medium, and light—plus several kinds of tea available, and a special French hot chocolate."

They all sounded good, especially the cocoa. In anticipation of their date, she hadn't eaten much today. Maybe it wouldn't ruin her appetite. "I'll have the hot chocolate."

"I'll be back with your drinks in a few minutes, ready to take your orders." He hurried off and disappeared into the dimness of a hallway.

Malcolm reached across the table and took her hand. "They have a menu, but I always ask what the specials are before I look there. Is that all right with you?"

"Yes." The warmth of his fingers encasing hers created a connection she didn't want to break.

"It might take a few minutes to fix the chocolate. We can talk until he gets back." Malcolm didn't let go of her hand. It felt so nice in hers.

The low lights and the soft music playing in the background enhanced the feeling of intimacy. Alanza enjoyed the ambiance. *What a perfect place for a first date.*

"So what do you want to talk about?" The rhythm of Malcolm's words and the rich bass tones of his voice surrounded her.

The question surprised her though. What did she want to know about him? *Everything.*

"MacGregor is a Scottish name. How long has your family been in the U.S.?" The words popped out of her mouth before she had time to think.

Malcolm laughed. "Yes, my family is full-blooded Scottish, but we've been in the U.S. since the 1700s."

"That's a long time. I didn't know any Scots settled here that long ago."

Malcolm gave Alanza's fingers a gentle squeeze. "In the 1700s, the English were trying to take the land away from the Highlanders. The Lairds were the landowners. I'm actually a direct descendent of one of the Lairds."

She smiled and took a sip of water. "That's amazing. I don't know my family history that far back."

"A lot of things brought the Scots here and they found North Carolina similar to the highlands. Taxes on the land were raised to exorbitant amounts by the English and the English defeated the Scots in the battle of Culloden in 1745. By immigrating to the colonies, they received land grants. My grandparents still live on the MacGregor land grant in North Carolina. We all return for special occasions. Especially the Highland Games."

Marcel approached with a tray. Malcolm let go of her hand. *Aw...*

"Here you are, Miss Cantalamessa." The waiter placed a large, steaming, frothy cup with whipped cream and curled, chocolate slivers in front of her.

"This looks wonderful." She took a sip. "And it tastes wonderful, too." Even that small sip began to warm her from the inside out.

"And Mr. MacGregor, here's your good ol' Texas Dr Pepper. Are you ready to order?"

"Not quite. I first want to hear what tonight's special is before we decide." Malcolm leaned back in his chair.

Despite having no pad or menu, Marcel had no trouble sharing that information. "Tonight, we have Beef Wellington. The crust is so flaky and the meat so tender, you almost won't need to chew it. The pâté inside is a savory blend of roasted red peppers, cream cheese, and capers. The special comes with grilled young asparagus spears on a bed of creamy polenta in a buttery sauce. At least, that's what the chef calls it. I think it's really just creamy, fine-ground grits."

Malcolm and Alanza both laughed. Malcolm turned to her. "Does that sound good, or do you want to order off the regular menu?"

"I'd love to try the Beef Wellington. My mouth was watering just thinking about it." She smiled up at Marcel. "You had me at flaky crust."

"Two Beef Wellingtons, please. Thank you, Marcel."

They enjoyed their beverages for a moment, listening to the music.

"I have another question, Malcolm. How did your family get from North Carolina to Texas?"

Malcolm smiled at her. "To tell you all about it would take all night and most of the day tomorrow. After the colonies became the United States of America, the frontier gradually moved farther and farther west, and the MacGregor clan grew along with the country. Some are all the way out in California. My immediate family ended up in Texas in the late 1800s. And we love it here."

She took another drink of her delicious hot dark chocolate. It warmed her clear to her toes. "How interesting. I don't think many people know about their family's history that far back. You should write a book for your descendents."

He gave her a bit of a wicked smile. "I don't have any descendants... yet."

I'd like to help you with that. Heat crept up her neck and poured into her cheeks. She hoped he'd think it was because she was feeling warmer and not blushing.

MALCOLM LOVED THE feeling of intimacy this private table gave them. The more time he spent with Alanza, the more his heart yearned for her to be his wife...and soon. Of course, it would have to be soon if she was moving with him to Australia in late January. He knew he couldn't push her too fast, but he didn't want to tell her about Australia until she had developed feelings for him. At least, they were moving that direction.

The food was everything Marcel said it would be. While he enjoyed every bite, he was more interested in watching Alanza's enjoyment play across her lovely face. Oh, how he wanted to kiss those cherry red lips! It was far too soon. *But there's so little time!*

Her every movement was graceful. A delight to watch.

"This is even more delicious than Marcel said." She touched her napkin lightly to her lips. "I don't think I've ever had a Beef Wellington this good. Of course, I haven't eaten it often. And I've never tried making it myself. I know there's a lot of prep work involved."

He placed his fork on the edge of his plate. "I'm kind of a foodie. I like finding places that have delicious, unique entrees and charming décor. This place is one of my favorites."

"Good." She flashed him a bright smile. "Maybe we can come here again. I'd like to try some of their other specials, maybe even get a look at the menu." She winked at him.

Oh, so she wants to see me again! He took her hand and gently squeezed her fingers. "I'd like that a lot."

Marcel stopped by their table. "Did you save room for dessert?"

Before Malcolm could answer, Alanza placed her hand on her stomach. "I know you must have wonderful desserts, but the meal was so delicious, I ate every bit of it. I couldn't touch another thing."

Malcolm gave her an indulgent smile. "Don't worry. We can come back again and have a dessert... or even come just for dessert."

"Of course." Marcel once again slipped down the hallway.

Soon he returned with a small tray, the bill upside down on it. Malcolm pulled out his credit card and laid it on top without looking at the total.

Marcel murmured, "Thank you," and left again.

After everything was taken care of, Malcolm slid Alanza's chair out from the table. They went toward the back door, and he claimed their coats. After holding hers open for her, he kept his hands on her shoulders a little longer than seemed necessary, but she didn't mind. He helped her button up before donning his own warm coat.

Soon they were headed toward her apartment.

"Tell me about your family. I'd like to know where they came from."

She looked out the window, then turned back to him. "Our story isn't nearly as interesting as your family's. I'm not sure when the Italian side of the family first came to America. I do know it was before the turn of the twentieth century."

He glanced toward her for a moment. "That's a good long time."

She smiled. "A lot of people were emigrating in the late nineteenth century. But the most interesting part of my family history is about the romance between my father and mother."

"Really? Why is that?" Malcolm was glad he hadn't turned the radio on when they got in the car. He wanted to know all he could about Alanza, her family, and her life.

"My father went to Brazil on spring break when he was a senior in college." A secret smile crept across her face.

"Brazil? That was unusual for his generation, wasn't it?" He slowed the car a little, so she could tell more of the story before they reached her apartment.

"You've heard the song, 'The Girl from Ipanema,' haven't you?"

He nodded. He'd heard several versions of that song and he always liked the bossa nova beat. The melody was an easy one to learn and the lyrics were romantic.

"My mother is from Brazil. She loved the beach. The first time Poppa saw her was near sunset as she walked along the shore. The words of the song fit her so well. She is tall, as tall as I am, and as tall as Poppa is. If she wears high heels, she towers over him, but he likes that. Of course, because of all the time she spent at the beach, she was very tan, and he says she's the loveliest woman he's ever seen. After he came home, they corresponded for about a month. He returned to Brazil, and when he came home a month later, she was his wife."

Alanza pulled the collar of her coat up around her neck and gave a satisfied smile.

"You're right. That's some story." Malcolm's heart beat a little faster. Maybe her parents wouldn't be opposed to a quick marriage, since they had a short courtship themselves. That was good. "I haven't seen your mother, have I? Does she work at the restaurant?"

Alanza thought back for a moment. "I'm not sure. She does work at the restaurant sometimes and I think she has been there when you've been in. But she might not have come into the front of the restaurant. She's out-of-town right now, in New York City, with a show at an upscale art gallery. She's a well-known artist."

He turned into the parking lot of her apartment. "Is anyone else in your family artistic?"

She cleared her throat. "Well, I am. Mamma and I worked together on the murals at the restaurant."

"Those are wonderful. I've enjoyed looking at them while I'm waiting for my food. They're so detailed." He stopped the car. "I look forward to meeting your mother and seeing more of her art... and yours."

5

Alanza watched Malcolm hurry around the car to open her door. None of the guys she dated in college did that. She hadn't known what she was missing. Being treated like a princess increased her appreciation for this tall redhead.

The night was still young. Should she ask him in? Would he think she wanted more from him? What she really wanted was to continue talking so she could get to know him better. He fascinated her. *Maybe I should ask him about his family's Highland Games. I'm sure there's a lot he could tell me.*

When he opened her door, more cold wind whistled into the car, and she hurried to get out. Malcolm quickly gathered her close and they walked up the steps to the front door in tandem, his bulk shielding her from most of the fierce wind.

Her hands were so cold, she fumbled with the keys, trying to unlock her apartment door.

"May I?" He spoke very close to her ear. A delicious shiver, that had nothing to do with the cold wind, rushed down her spine.

Alanza nodded and handed him her keys. Seemingly without looking, he quickly had the door open.

She stepped inside. "Would you like to come in for a while?" She did her best to sound casual, so he wouldn't get the wrong idea.

A wide smile spread across his face and lit up his eyes. "I'd like that." He followed her and closed the door behind them. "I was hoping you'd want to talk some more."

She hung her coat in the front hallway closet. "I don't have the fancy things they did at the restaurant, but I can offer you plain hot chocolate with marshmallows on top. Or coffee or hot tea." She smiled up at him. "No Dr Pepper, I'm afraid."

"Hot chocolate sounds good to me." Malcolm glanced around her living room. "I like your apartment. It looks really homey." He took off his coat, and she hung it on an empty hanger in the closet.

"When I graduated from college, I didn't want to move back home, so my family surprised me with this apartment with the first year's rent paid. I wanted it to be homey. You should've seen all the shopping I did to make it fit my personality."

"I'd have enjoyed shopping with you." He smiled at her.

"Yeah, right!" Her incredulous retort made him laugh. "None of the guys in my family would be caught dead shopping with us girls."

Alanza headed toward her kitchen. "It won't take me long to heat up the chocolate."

He followed her. "Do you need help?"

"No, but we can visit while I make it."

She went to the fridge to gather the ingredients, he pulled out a chair from the table, turned it around, and straddled it with his arms folded along the back.

"Tell me more about the Highland Games." She poured milk into a pan, put the stove burner on low heat, and slowly stirred in some cocoa. "I've heard of them before, but never knew anyone who actually participated."

He laughed. "I'm a Scottish highlander. My ancestors lived up in the crags and mountains. Well, they wouldn't be considered mountains by people who've seen the Alps or the Rockies, but they divided us from the lowlanders who lived closer to the English. Highlanders are strong men of valor. They've always had contests that tested their skills."

While Alanza stirred the cocoa, she listened to Malcolm's deep baritone voice, wondering about his accent. It seemed to be a curious blend of Texan, Mountain Southern, and Scottish brogue. She liked it very much. She could imagine him in a kilt with a tartan cloak slung over his broad shoulders. She'd bet anything that he won every contest he entered.

He stood and slid the chair back under the table. His presence took up most of the space in the small kitchen. His breathing stole more than his share of the air in the room. Was it the large meal she had eaten or something else that made her feel faint? She had never fainted in her life.

She added both honey and sugar to the warming chocolatey milk. Now she had to pay close attention to keep it from scalding.

He leaned back against the counter near the stovetop. The scent of his intoxicating aftershave surrounded her. *Or was it cologne?* It was woodsy, with a touch of spice. And warmth. Lots of warmth.

"When the Scots moved to America, they brought their contests with them. Several places here in the U.S. still hold Highland Games. There's actually one not far from here." He put his hands in his pants pockets and shifted his weight from one foot to the other. "Maybe we can attend them sometime. They're usually in the spring or summer."

So this wasn't just a one-time date for him. Good. "I'd like that."

She took the pan off the burner, dropped tiny marshmallows into the waiting over-sized mugs, and filled them with the fragrant hot chocolate. "Do you want to drink it here, or would you rather go in the living room? The sofa is more comfortable."

"Whatever you want to do." His honeyed tone wrapped around her like a warm blanket.

She handed a mug to him, picked up her own, along with coasters and two napkins, and headed into the living room. He followed.

After watching Alanza get comfortable on the couch, Malcolm sat close to her… but not too close. What a picture she made leaning back into the fluffy pillows with her legs pulled up beside her.

Thank you, Lord, for planning this woman for my wife. He really needed to handle the next several days with wisdom. He was afraid that if he told her everything at once, she'd be over-whelmed. And might reject him outright. After his night with the Lord, he couldn't let that happen. And he was quickly falling in love with her.

He didn't feel right about keeping his promotion and the need to temporarily move to Australia from her, but that would be a lot to take in all at once. *What do I say? I don't want to dump a lot of information on her but I need to let her know somehow. It has to be soon. January isn't far off.*

He leaned forward. After taking a swig of the delicious chocolate, he set his mug on the coaster she'd placed on the coffee table. "I'm glad you wanted to talk more tonight."

Her eyes widened, as if she wondered where he was going with this discussion.

Without thinking, Malcolm plunged right in. "I'm ready to settle down and get married. I know this is sudden, but if there's anything about me you wouldn't want in a husband, I'd like you to tell me."

A gasp escaped her pretty mouth. She blinked, then set her mug down. "I don't know what to say."

"Oh, I don't expect any kind of answer tonight."

His quick response helped her to visibly relax. She picked up her chocolate again.

Now that it was cooler, he took a larger swig of his own. "This tastes really good. Like my family always had when I was growing up."

She leaned deeper into the cushions. "I've always liked this kind, too."

Now they were talking without really communicating. He felt a distance between them he hadn't felt before. Was it time to go for broke?

"Alanza, when I asked your father if I could date you, I told him it was with marriage in mind."

A blush rushed into her cheeks. "Nothing was said to me about marriage. We barely know each other."

"I know." *Lord, help me. I know I'm not handling this right.*

He got up and went to her front hallway closet. After pulling the wrapped package from the large pocket of his overcoat, he came back and sat beside her. Once again, not too close. He didn't want to make matters worse. Nothing was going the way he'd envisioned it would. But he went ahead anyway. Hoping. Praying.

"I brought you a gift." He held out the package.

"Why?" Alanza's eyes glittered as she looked from his face to the gift—wrapped in shiny gold paper with a red and green bow—and back to his face again, studying him, her eyes narrowing. "It's not Christmas yet."

"I know." He cleared his throat, which suddenly felt tight. "It's not a Christmas gift. It's just something I had made especially for you."

Malcolm set it on the table in front of her. Alanza stared at it, and he wished he knew what was going through her mind. Picking up his mug, he took another large swig of his cocoa—and was so nervous, he nearly choked on it.

The room felt as if it had expanded, adding space between them. This was turning into the most awkward date he'd ever had. *Lord, help me.*

Finally, she reached for the package and carefully removed every piece of tape and the plaid ribbon, laying them on the table. She lifted the lid as if she thought whatever was in the box might jump out and bite her.

Malcolm was almost hyperventilating, a strange, new, unwelcome experience. He started to turn away, then decided to keep watching her.

Alanza laid the lid beside the tape and ribbon and reached into the box. After lifting the hair ornament out, she turned it over and studied it a moment.

"Malcolm, this is beautiful. Thank you." Confusion still covered her face like a veil, hiding her warm smile.

"That is the MacGregor tartan."

Once again, her eyes widened.

Lord, how will I ever live through this? His stomach roiled as if he'd been exercising too much after a large meal.

He reached toward her and paused. He felt reassured when she reached over to hold his hand. That felt better. "I want you to think about what I asked you. When you put this in your hair, it will let me know that there's not anything about me you wouldn't want in a husband. Okay?"

She nodded and kept her hand in his. That gave him hope.

MALCOLM LEFT SOON afterward. *Okay, was that a fiasco or...?* On the drive home, he went over every word he said to her—and everything she said to him. How could he have handled it differently? And how could he court her and convince her to marry him before going off to Australia?

So many variables, he couldn't imagine all of them. When would be the right time to tell her about his promotion? How soon could he tell her everything without scaring her away? How could he get her to fall in love with him the way he already felt he loved her?

When he arrived at his apartment, Malcolm was glad Eric was not there. He didn't want to talk to his roommate when he wasn't even sure what he was feeling just then. After what Eric said last night, Malcolm wasn't ready to share anything else about him and Alanza with his supposed best friend.

He and Eric were long-time best friends, even though they didn't see eye to eye on everything. For instance, Eric sometimes stuck his nose into Malcolm's business. And his roommate didn't share his deep relationship with the Lord. He would never understand about the night Malcolm spent in prayer about his relationship with Alanza. Eric didn't know anything about listening for God's *still small voice.*

Malcolm would cling to the things God told him Wednesday night.

Lord, I don't know how You are going to bring this about in such a short time, but I will trust in You and listen for Your promptings every day.

ALANZA SHUT THE door after Malcolm left, locked it, and leaned against it. She was pretty sure a Scottish man didn't give a gift with his tartan to a woman unless he was extremely interested in her...like about to be engaged or something like that. And his question still threw her.

Is there anything about him that I wouldn't want in a husband? After just one date, it was too soon to think about Malcolm in those terms. But he was certainly the nicest, most polite, and most protective man she'd ever gone out with. And there was certainly chemistry between them. *Romantic tension.* That's what some romance writers called it. So far, there was nothing about him Alanza didn't like or wouldn't want in a husband. *But I don't know him that well. How am I supposed to answer that question after one night and a few conversations at the restaurant?*

And she certainly didn't want to start searching for something not to like. If she watched every little thing he did and analyzed every little thing he said, it could ruin any chance of something more developing between them. She didn't want to ruin their budding relationship. She wanted to enjoy it and let things take their natural course.

After walking through her apartment to turn off the lights, Alanza got ready for bed. Her conversation with Malcolm over the hot chocolate turned over and over in her mind.

She'd had friends at the University of Texas Arlington who had trusted men—and shouldn't have. At first, they seemed like nice, friendly guys. Then they showed their true colors as the relationships progressed. Rude remarks. Trying to force themselves on her friends. What if this happened with Malcolm? They hadn't known each other long enough and she didn't know enough about him.

After slipping between the flannel sheets under her thick comforter, she tried to go to sleep. But imaginary scenarios kept flitting through her mind. She tossed and turned for a long time before falling into slumber troubled by weird dreams. Once, she woke up and whispered into the darkened room. "God, what am I supposed to do?"

She wished for an audible answer from God, but there was no still small voice to disrupt the stillness in her room, just the usual night sounds. The fridge humming. The clock ticking. Finally, her thoughts quieted and she slept soundly.

6

Saturday – Eleven Days Before Christmas

An early morning text from Malcolm woke Alanza on Saturday. She didn't have to work this weekend, so she'd planned to sleep late. His words on her phone illuminated the darkness.

"Are you awake yet? Do you have plans for today? Would you like to do something with me?"

Three questions. Which should she answer first?

"Yes, I'm awake."

She didn't have to tell him he woke her up.

"Today is my Saturday off work. What do you have in mind?"

Give him a question to answer. She got out of bed and turned on the light. *Might as well get up. So much for sleeping in. Maybe he has something fun planned.*

Immediately, his answering text arrived.

"Have breakfast with me? Then we can have fun all day."

What does he consider "fun"? Hmmm. It really would be nice to spend a day with him. And maybe figure out an answer to his question.

"Okay. Give me 45 minutes."

"Great," came his quick reply.

Alanza went to her closet to start looking for something to wear. She glanced at the tartan bow on her dresser. After he dropped that bombshell on her last night, the question he'd asked kept coming back to her mind. So far, Malcolm *was* everything she wanted in a husband—maybe more. But would that continue?

There was no getting around the fact that he was handsome. And taller than her, which was a plus. His rich auburn hair wasn't really curly, but also wasn't straight. It was thick and wavy and complemented his strong, masculine features. She'd never had a desire to run her fingers through a man's hair before... but Malcolm's hair? Yes... *Alanza, stop daydreaming.*

She took too long trying to decide what to wear. Finally, she chose thick leggings and a knee-length pullover sweater over a cozy, long-sleeved T-shirt. She had to hurry showering and fixing her hair and makeup, or she wouldn't be ready when he arrived.

At exactly 45 minutes since his last text, the doorbell rang. She'd just finished pulling on her knee-high boots. Today wasn't supposed to be any warmer than yesterday. If they were going to be outdoors much, she wanted to keep warm.

She opened her front door, and Malcolm's smile captured her. "Good morning. You look great." His tone carried the feel of a caress.

"Thank you. Come in." Feeling the heat creep into her cheeks, she turned away to get her long coat from the closet.

He entered and closed the door behind him and helped her into her coat. "I hope you're hungry. I'm going to take you to my favorite breakfast café."

"What café?" She buttoned up every button and wrapped a warm scarf around her neck.

He led the way out her door and to his car. "Have you heard of Oldwest Café?"

She slid into the seat and reached for the seatbelt. "On 121?"

"That's the one." He closed her door and went around to his side.

When he was seated, she elaborated. "I've seen it before and wondered about it. I'll be glad to try it out."

He backed out of the parking space. "The food is really good, and the décor is interesting. Lots of western items. John Wayne things. There's even a horse down at one end of the building."

She laughed. "A horse?"

"It's not real, but it's life-sized and very authentic looking."

"I can hardly wait."

This early on a Saturday, the parking lot wasn't quite full, but a lot of people beat them there. She hoped they wouldn't have to wait long to get their food. After talking about breakfast earlier, she was feeling hungry.

The hostess said there was a fifteen-minute wait, so Malcolm took her to see the horse and all of the John Wayne memorabilia. The fifteen minutes went fast, because before they were finished browsing the posters, the hostess called Malcolm's name.

As they studied the menus, Alanza glanced up at him. "I only see the breakfast menu and one page of lunch items. Aren't they open for dinner?"

"No. Just breakfast and lunch." He closed his menu.

"Do you know what you'll be having?" She still studied the offerings.

"I come here often, so I'll have my usual. What do you want to try?"

She pointed to a spot on the menu. "I love Eggs Benedict. That lady sitting behind you ordered it, and the waitress just set it down. It looks delicious."

MALCOLM LOVED WATCHING Alanza enjoy her breakfast.

"I wasn't sure about ordering this in a café. It's kind of upscale for a place like this. But they must have an excellent chef in the kitchen." She took another bite and closed her eyes, savoring the flavors. "I've never had better."

He pushed his empty plate away and picked up the bill. "I'll pay while you finish, so we can get on with our other fun today."

When he glanced back at Alanza, she took another bite and seemed to be puzzling over something. Maybe wondering what other fun he was talking about. He hoped she would be surprised and happy when she found out he was taking her to one of the best places to shop in Southlake.

He drove on up 121 to 114, then around to Southlake Town Square. She watched every turn he took.

"So what's so much fun out here?" Her smile took the sting out of the question.

"You'll see."

Alanza looked all around Southlake Town Square as Malcolm made his way to the west parking garage. "There are so many different kinds of stores and restaurants here. I've only passed by 114 and Southlake Boulevard. I didn't realize just how diverse it is inside the square."

When they left the car and headed across the street, he pulled her close and tried to take the brunt of the wind. He guided her into the Apple store.

"What are we doing here? Do you need to buy something?"

He nodded. "Yes, a gift. Let's look at the iPads."

"Is it a Christmas gift?"

He didn't want to tell her a lie. "Not really."

"Who's it for?" She was persistent.

"A woman."

"Someone in your family?"

Something like that. I hope. He pretended not to hear her, engrossed in looking around the store. They walked through the displays until they saw the iPads. "I want you to help me find the best one." Many were on display, with so many options, he wasn't sure where to start.

Alanza's eyes sparkled. "Ooo, look at this one. It's the only one with that rose-gold color."

Malcolm looked at the specs. "Hmm, it does look good. It's got a nice camera, and it comes with either Wi-Fi or Wi-Fi and cellular. It would be more useful with both. I think I'll get the one with 256 gig hard drive."

Alanza kept playing with the display model while he paid for the tablet and a digital stylus pen for it.

When he returned to where she stood, Alanza looked up. "I've never tried an iPad. It does lots more than my old tablet did. Of course, it costs way more than mine did, too." She placed the display back on the stand. "Where are we going now?"

He led her out of the store.

"We'll go anywhere you want to." Malcolm looked around. "Here's a map of all the stores."

Alanza unwrapped her scarf. "The wind has died down. It doesn't feel so cold anymore. I'm game to check out a few places."

"Your wish is my command." He led her back into the garage and locked the package he carried in the trunk. "Now my hands are free to carry any bags you need me to."

They headed back out into the open air. He took her hand and they walked along the sidewalk, window shopping.

"You're really special, Malcolm. None of the guys in my family would be caught dead shopping with a girl."

He hoped she'd begin to appreciate who he really was. They spent the rest of the morning going to the stores that interested Alanza. He loved watching her as she shopped. Her eyes gleamed when she saw something she wanted. He knew she was having fun—but so was he. Spending time with her, doing things that made her happy, did something to his heart. Somehow, it illustrated for him the way God loves everyone. *He will take great delight in you.* And Malcolm thought about a verse he'd read from the Bible this morning. *Let all that you do be done with love.*

His heart expanded every time Alanza laughed. He didn't know how often she went shopping or spent a lot of money. Sometimes, she would show him something she was buying for a family member for Christmas. A few times, she bought things for herself. She was especially happy when she found something she wanted at a really good price. He finally understood why women enjoy shopping and he rejoiced with her.

After several hours, they returned to the parking garage with more bags. Good thing the Beamer had a nice large trunk.

"Are you getting hungry?" He sure was. Shopping was hard work.

"A little."

"Lots of good places to eat near here." Malcolm pulled the map out of his coat pocket and handed it to her.

Alanza studied it. "I've never been to the Cheesecake Factory. Maybe it won't be too busy since it's past one o'clock."

"I can pull the car around to the parking lot near there, if you want me to."

"We can walk." She took his hand in hers. "I've heard from friends that the food is good, and there's a lot of it. Besides, I'm sure I'll have to try some of the cheesecake." She grinned.

He was overjoyed that she was the one to take his hand this time. Maybe she was warming up to the idea that they were destined to be together.

"If we want to order the same thing, maybe we could split it, so you can save more room for dessert," he suggested. He knew he could eat a whole meal and a dessert, but maybe she couldn't.

"Or maybe I could take half of mine home to eat later." She stopped on the edge of the curb then looked both ways before plunging into the street. "That way, you could have enough to eat. I know how hungry men can get. And a big muscular guy like you needs a lot of fuel."

Her laughter made his heart beat faster. Her joking let him know she was feeling more comfortable with him. *Thank you, Lord.*

WHEN THEY REACHED Alanza's apartment late Saturday afternoon, she was worn out. She'd never spent so much time shopping, nor had she had so much fun doing it. The best thing about it was sharing it with Malcolm. He'd been a good sport about all the shopping and he didn't look a bit tired.

He opened her car door. "I'll help you carry in all your loot."

"That's very kind of you. Thanks."

While he went to the trunk, she unlocked the apartment door. She looked back at him as he walked up her front steps with both arms full.

"Here." He set most of them on the coffee table with a few on the sofa. "I'll get the rest, Alanza. No need for you to go back out into the cold."

She closed the door behind him and watched through the picture window. The more time she spent with this man, the more he enthralled her. He was so close to capturing her heart. *Yes, he's charming. Yes, he's so sweet and fun to be with. But everything is happening way too fast!*

She opened the door again.

"This is the last of the packages." He handed them to her this time. "I'll go back and get the leftover food from lunch."

While he was gone, she moved the shopping bags to her bedroom. She'd have time to go through them when he left... but she wasn't ready for him to go yet.

He opened the front door and handed her the packaged food. Of course, he had eaten every bite of his meal and dessert.

She flashed him a quick smile. "Would you like some hot chocolate before you head home?"

He grinned. "Do you have to ask? You bet I do!" He hung his coat in the closet as if it were its regular place. This time, he didn't follow her to the kitchen. She hurried as fast as she could creating the frothy hot drink.

She carried a large mug in each hand when she returned. He sat in her rocker-recliner, watching her. She didn't see the package on the coffee table until she almost reached the sofa. Her gaze shot toward him. *What is that?* She hadn't seen him do any shopping for himself today. The box was covered with gold foil paper. A large gold bow almost covered the lid.

He leaned forward and received his cup of chocolate. He blew on the surface and took a tiny sip. "That's too hot to drink right now." He set it on the table. "I have another present for you."

She set her chocolate down then sat against the cushions on the sofa, just staring at the shiny box. "It's not Christmas."

He nodded. "I know."

"Malcolm, you're very sweet, but you shouldn't give me presents without a reason."

He smiled. "I have a reason."

She waited for him to elaborate on his statement. When he didn't, she reached for the box. Slowly lifting the lid, she peeked inside. *The iPad.*

"This was for me?" She didn't pick it up. "When did you have it wrapped?"

"I wrapped the box to put it in before I left home."

"So you planned to buy this for me before we left. Why?"

She couldn't accept such an expensive gift. The tartan hair ornament was one thing, but this was much, much more. Of course, it might not be more important to him than the clip. *Why is he doing this for me?*

"Last night, you mentioned there had been an accident at work that crushed your tablet and you said you hadn't replaced it yet." His intense gaze zeroed in on her hands.

What could she do? "I can't accept anything this expensive from you."

"I know what you're thinking. It's not a big deal, really. It's just a gift from me to you. No strings attached."

Maybe he understood how those strings attached to the hair clip had her tied up in knots.

"Haven't any of your friends ever given you a gift for no particular reason?"

She couldn't think of a single time when that happened, so she shook her head.

"We *are* friends, aren't we?"

All she could do was nod.

"So I'm a friend giving you a gift for no special reason. When a friend gives you a gift and you refuse it, you're denying that friend the opportunity to experience the blessings from giving a gift. Would you really deny me blessings?"

She didn't have an answer to that. "Okay." She took the computer out of the box.

Malcolm moved to the sofa and went over its features with her. They had some fun drawing sketches with the digital pen. She laughed at his doodles while her artistry amazed him. They also downloaded the YouVersion Bible app.

After they finished their cocoa, he stood up. "I should get going. Would you go to church with me tomorrow?"

"Where do you go to church?" The words came out as a whisper.

"Way of Life."

A smile lit her face. "My family goes there, too."

"Which campus?" They both spoke at once.

He gestured for her to go first.

"We attend the Arlington campus."

He nodded. "I usually go to the Grapevine campus. Would you let me take you there tomorrow?"

"Yes. What time?"

"Would you rather go to the eleven o'clock or the one o'clock service?"

She smiled at him. "If we go to the eleven o'clock one, we'll be finished at a good time to eat lunch."

"That works for me. Think about where you want to go out to eat and tell me tomorrow morning when I pick you up."

She gave his hand a little squeeze. "I enjoyed today, Malcolm. Thank you."

He went to the closet to get his coat then turned back toward her as he put it on. "I had fun today, too. And I'll be looking forward to seeing you tomorrow."

She watched his car as he pulled out of her parking lot.

Another day with Malcolm—and with You, Lord. Thank you.

7

Sunday – Ten Days Before Christmas

Strange dreams flitted through Alanza's sleep Saturday night. When she'd awakened the first time, she couldn't remember exactly what she dreamed, but whatever it was left her with an unsettled feeling. She got up and went to take a Tylenol PM, hoping that would help her sleep soundly the rest of the night.

Once again, she woke with a start, not understanding what had caused it. Then snippets of the dreams flashed through her mind. Malcolm had been in them. First, he came toward her, but at some point, he turned and walked away from her. He didn't turn around even though she cried out to him. The turmoil she felt after he left the last time must have lingered.

She dropped to her knees beside her bed and prayed. *Dear Lord, please calm my restless spirit. Help me understand what is happening and give me peace and wisdom. And I thank You, Lord, for all of the blessings You have given me. Amen.* This time, when she climbed back into bed, closed her eyes, and pulled the covers higher around her neck, the sleep that claimed her wasn't haunted by lingering memories of bad dreams.

The alarm awakened her in plenty of time to get ready for church. Immediately, her eyes were drawn to the tartan hair clip on her dresser. She really wanted to wear it, but since Malcolm attached such significance to it, she couldn't. *He'd probably think I'm ready to marry him!* Her new green wool knit dress and a red scarf would look awesome with it. *Christmassy.* Still in her nightgown, she turned away from the clip and went to the kitchen to have some coffee with a bagel and cream cheese.

When she was ready to get dressed, she decided on the green knit dress and red scarf anyway, along with her knee-high black boots. Christmas was her favorite time of the year, so she had a lot of seasonal jewelry. After she had applied makeup and fixed her hair, she pulled out the scarf and a gold snowflake-shaped brooch studded with pearls. Draping the scarf just right, she attached it at one shoulder with the pearl pin. The perfect look for the holidays. With one last longing gaze at the hair clip, she headed into the living room. *Malcolm will be here any minute.*

What if he asked about the hair bow? What should I say? She hoped he wouldn't, because she wasn't ready to make that kind of commitment. *But I don't want to drive him away either. He IS the kind of man I would want as a husband. At least, he has been so far. But I need more intel. Has he been his true self or is he just trying to impress me, for whatever reason?*

Her doorbell chime pealed through the apartment. She loved the "Für Elise" melody it played. She hurried to the door and pulled it open. Malcolm's eyes rested on her face with so much affection in his expression, she could feel her heart beat faster.

"Come in while I get my coat and my purse and make sure the iPad is in it." She'd use that during the Bible readings. She could even take notes on it if she wanted to.

He entered and shut the door behind him.

When she turned from getting her coat out of the closet, his gaze was on her hair, and she detected a hint of disappointment. A twinge of guilt pinched her. She really didn't want to disappoint him, but she was too conflicted to give the answer he so desired from her. How could he expect it from her after only two dates?

Yes, Alanza had heard about so-called "love at first sight," but she'd never really believed in it. Except for her parents. Their courtship had been short, with part of it long distance, and they'd been happily married for over twenty-six years.

Malcolm took her coat and held it open for her. When he pulled it up over her shoulders, he was careful not to disturb her scarf or the pin. *He's so gentle and endearing. Almost too good to be true.* She was going to have to decide if she could trust him with her heart… and soon.

"You look especially beautiful this morning." His warm breath disturbed a few hairs near the back of her neck.

"Thank you." She looked him up and down. "And you clean up really well, too, Mr. MacGregor."

He laughed. "Ready to go?"

MALCOLM TRIED NOT to show his disappointment when Alanza didn't wear the hair bow. He'd love to have her wearing a bit of his tartan.

He had left the engine running so the car would be warm for her. This cold snap was holding on longer than usual.

After he helped Alanza into the car, he went to his side and got in. "Green is a very good color for you."

Was the blush in her cheeks from the cold or from his words?

"Thank you." She finished buckling her seatbelt and turned back toward him. Her bright smile took away the momentary disappointment he'd felt.

He pulled out of her apartment parking lot and headed toward his church. "Did you decide where you want to go eat after church?"

"I'm not that familiar with the restaurants near your church campus." She settled her purse on her lap. "I don't go out that way very often, and even then, I'm not usually looking for a place to eat." She laughed. "With my parents owning a restaurant, we don't eat out much to begin with, unless it's some cuisine we don't do, like Thai."

Traffic was heavier than usual. He wondered why. Soon the reason appeared on the highway ahead of them. He saw it far enough away to change his plans. Getting stuck in traffic caused by an accident would make them late for the service. He pulled off onto the access road.

"Is there some shortcut to the church I don't know about?"

He glanced at Alanza. She was looking at him instead of the road ahead. "There's a large wreck up ahead. I'm taking another way, so we'll be on time."

"I hope no one is hurt." The concern in her voice touched his heart.

"Maybe we could pray for the people involved."

She nodded just as he turned onto another street that would take them where they wanted to go. "Since you're driving, I'll pray out loud so we can be in agreement."

One more reason to love her. Their shared faith in God.

Alanza bowed her head and closed her eyes. That couldn't shut out the small part of the crash that she had seen. It looked like there were at least four vehicles involved. With such a major accident, chances were that at least one person was injured.

"Dear Lord, my heart aches for the people involved in that wreck. What little I saw looked awful. I'm afraid the people involved are either badly injured... or maybe someone died. We have no way to know about whether they know You or not. If they don't, I pray that someone will introduce You to them, maybe even while they are being treated. For those who are injured, we pray for wisdom for the doctors and other medical personnel who care for them. We pray that You will ease their pain and that they are able to recover quickly. If someone was killed, we pray for their loved ones as they face this loss. We pray that it will bring them closer to You. For those who need miracles, whether physical, financial, or emotional, we pray that You bring those miracles to them. Give them all the peace that passes understanding and lift them in Your mighty arms close to Your heart. In Jesus's name, amen."

"Amen." Malcolm's gentle voice agreed with her.

She opened her eyes, raised her head, and looked around as Malcolm turned into the large church parking lot, which was almost full. "Wow, there are a lot of people here. I guess I didn't know this building was so large."

He stopped the car in the lane near the front door. "I'm going to let you out, so you won't have to walk so far in the cold wind. Wait for me inside near the front door. It won't take me long to park the car."

His thoughtfulness once again warmed her heart. "Thank you."

She picked up her purse and opened the door. Only a few steps took her inside the welcoming warmth.

Two women, an older redhead and a tall young blonde, stood just inside the door to greet her. They introduced themselves and Alanza did the same.

The older woman smiled at her. "Cantalamessa? Like the Italian restaurant on Highway 10?"

"The same. My family owns it."

"We love to eat there. Actually, that's where we plan to have lunch today after church."

The younger woman shivered as more people came through the front door, so they moved farther into the lobby.

"Are you new to Way of Life Church?" she asked Alanza.

"My family are members, but I haven't been to this campus before." She glanced around at the walls of windows that let in lots of sunlight.

Groups of people clustered around the large lobby, the sound of happy voices music to her ears.

"Are you meeting someone here?"

"My, uh… my boyfriend is parking the car." *He is my boyfriend… kind of. At least we're dating.*

The blond woman glanced over Alanza's head. "There's a handsome hunk looking for someone. Is that him?"

Alanza turned around and Malcolm hurried toward her, his face lit up in a big smile. "Yes, it's him."

"Don't let that one get away. He's a keeper." The other woman finished just before Malcolm stopped beside Alanza. She hoped he hadn't heard what she said.

"There you are." He slipped his arm around her waist.

She turned back to her two greeters. "This is Malcolm MacGregor."

Malcolm's arm tightened around her a little. "Thanks for keeping her company, ladies. We should go in and find seats. The service is about to start."

THE SERVICE LASTED about an hour and a half. When it was over, people all around them greeted Malcolm, and he introduced Alanza to them. They welcomed her warmly. Soon they were able to make their way through the lobby to the front door.

"Do you want to wait here while I get the car?" He smiled down at her.

"Where did you park?"

They walked to the window and he pointed out his car in the back of the parking lot.

She glanced out the window, then back at him. "The trees aren't moving much, so it's not as windy. And the sun is out now. It's probably warmer. I'll just walk with you."

Sure enough, the sunshine warmed them a little. They walked hand in hand toward his car.

"What did you think about the service?"

She looked up at him. "Of course, we have the same sermon at all the campuses at the same time, and we have our own worship team and band, but it was so much bigger here. A larger worship team, a larger band, larger screens, more people. There's a certain vibe I haven't experienced before."

"So you liked it?"

They reached the car, and he unlocked it for her.

"Of course I did."

She slipped inside the car. Good, she seemed more relaxed than she was before church.

He went to the driver's side and joined her. "Did you decide what kind of food you want for lunch?"

"There are lots of places around here. But won't they be busy with such a large crowd getting out of church right now?" She slid her coat from her shoulders and left it against the back of her seat.

He started the car and got in line to exit the parking lot. "I have an idea. We're not far from where we went shopping yesterday at Southlake Town Square. Let's see if we can find somewhere to eat there. Then we can go to the Gaylord Hotel."

She raised her head and their gazes collided, an almost visible connection. "What?" *Please God I hope he's not suddenly getting the wrong ideas about me!*

"Have you ever seen ICE! at Gaylord Texan?"

Alanza's eyes brightened. "I've read about it, but I've never been there. Somehow I can't imagine choosing to go into some cold, icy place in the wintertime."

"Well, the temperature *has* gone up a little. And they have amazing Christmas decorations all over the place. We could go to ICE! then enjoy all there is to see there. We could make a day of it. The lights are awesome when the sun goes down."

"Do they let people just come in and sightsee without getting a hotel room?" She sounded doubtful.

"Of course, they do. The Gaylord is a destination as well as a hotel. Just wait and see. You'll love it."

8

*Y*ou won't want to go through ICE! in your Sunday clothes. Let's get something to eat, then I'll take you home to change." Malcolm loved Alanza's smile. "I have some casual clothes to wear in my duffel bag in the trunk."

"Okay."

"What kind of food are you hungry for?" He wanted to please her more than anything in the world.

"Mexican food or seafood." She shrugged. "I don't care which kind."

He glanced at the traffic ahead of them and turned back toward Southlake Town Center. "If you want seafood, I like Rockfish Grill on this side of 1709 or Bonefish Grill on the other side."

Alanza's laughter filled the car. "Really? Bonefish Grill? That's a funny name. And with you saying it alongside Rockfish Grill, that's just too hilarious. Which restaurant do you like better?"

"Both of them have good seafood. Rockfish has awesome seafood enchiladas. If you try that, you'll get both Mexican food and seafood." He smiled over at her. "I'll drive by and see if there's a parking space nearby."

He went around Town Hall and found a space right across the street from Rockfish. When they entered, there were only two parties ahead of them. *Unusual for a Sunday, but of course it was almost one o'clock.* It shouldn't take long to get a table. He removed his coat and helped Alanza out of hers. A couple sitting together on the waiting bench were called to their table.

He guided Alanza into the empty space and slid in beside her. They were very close, but she didn't seem to mind, and he sure didn't. *The closer to her, the better.* She settled against him, a wide smile on her face. The hostess offered them a menu, so they could have an idea of what they wanted before they were seated.

He opened it to the page with a picture of seafood enchiladas. "This is what I was talking about."

Alanza looked at the menu. "Mmm, looks yummy. What's in it?"

He held the menu closer to her so she could read it.

"Oh, I know I'm going to love that." She glanced up at him.

Her face was really close to his. Their gazes caught and once again, he felt such a strong connection with her. He hoped she did, too. She didn't look away until the hostess called them.

As they followed the woman to a booth, Alanza whispered to him, "It smells so good in here, it's making me hungrier."

"Good. We'll both need to eat plenty because we'll be doing a lot of walking and other things before we eat again."

MALCOLM CLEANED HIS plate, but Alanza asked for a takeout box for part of hers.

"If I don't finish what I eat, I always take the rest home. It keeps me from having to cook for myself, which gets a little tiresome. With what I took home from the Cheesecake Factory and this today, I'm set for a while."

They headed to her apartment.

Alanza led the way through her front door. "Down that way..." She gestured toward a door on the other side of the living room. "...is the other bedroom and bath. You can change in there."

"Thanks." Malcolm's long legs quickly carried him to the door.

She watched him, enjoying his enthusiasm. One more check on the plus side of the list about things she might want in a husband. And the negative side was still empty.

After donning jeans over her thick leggings, she pulled on Ugg boots. She seldom had an opportunity to wear them, but they'd come in handy, especially in the extreme cold. The soles should grip enough to keep her from sliding and falling on the icy floor. Her knee-length sweater over the long-sleeved T she'd worn the other day would keep her warm in most places. Instead of her dress coat, she brought out the jacket to her ski suit.

When she returned to the living room, she had to catch her breath when she saw Malcolm. Jeans and hiking boots with what looked like layered pullover sweaters accentuated his physique. His Sunday clothes were folded over his arm that held the strap of the duffel bag, and a ski jacket hung across the other shoulder, held only by his forefinger. He could have stepped from the cover of GQ Magazine.

A flock of hummingbirds took up residence in her stomach. She turned away before he could see the blush climb into her cheeks. "Good, looks like we're ready to go."

They quickly reached the entrance to the hotel property.

"Have you ever been to the Gaylord?" Malcolm turned down a street that passed a closed water park on the right, then crossed over a bridge.

"No, but we've driven past the entrance to Gaylord Trail when we've gone to Grapevine Mills to shop." Alanza gasped as they headed toward the main part of the hotel. "I've never been down here. I didn't realize it was so close to the lake."

Even on this cold winter day, several boats from the marina skimmed across the water. She couldn't imagine taking a boat out in this weather. At least, the lake wasn't frozen over.

As THEY DROVE around Gaylord Trail to get to the entrance of the hotel, Malcolm watched her out of the corner of his eyes. She looked like a little girl getting her first glimpse of the Christmas displays in department store windows. His heart expanded with more love for her, pleased he was the one to introduce her to the spectacle they would experience today.

Christmas decorations were everywhere. He was happy the nativity scene would have a prominent place in all of it.

After the ICE! personnel bundled them up in polar coats, they headed down a hallway to the entrance. He'd been afraid the place would be really crowded on the weekend, but it wasn't today. Maybe they came at just the right time, between crowds.

He gave Alanza his arm so she could hold on to him as they stepped on the frozen floor. As they entered the multicolored entry made of carved ice, she gasped and tightened her grip. This first blast of arctic air could be a shock. He watched her as her twinkling eyes roved around the imaginative displays.

"This is amazing. I've read about how this was created but I never imagined anything this beautiful." She walked a few steps then stopped again to study everything surrounding them.

Scenes from "The Night Before Christmas" were carved out of multi-colored ice and white ice.

"It's breathtaking." She stood until she shivered, and they moved on.

Malcolm pulled her against his side and slid his arm around her. Maybe that would help to keep her warm. Their breath hung in the nine-degree air that kept the two million pounds of ice from melting. After exploring the colorful displays, they reached the room with the nativity scene, carved out of crystal clear ice.

Alanza craned her neck to see the top of an angel that stood beside the nativity, at least ten feet tall. "That angel is awesome, Malcolm. Can you please stand close to it so I can get a picture of you and the angel?"

She had a hard time getting to her phone, but finally pulled it out of her pocket. As she tried to center it to get as much of the angel as she could and include Malcolm, another couple came up behind them.

"I can take a picture of both of you and the angel." The woman's friendly smile encompassed them.

"Thank you so much." Alanza handed over her phone and slipped under Malcolm's arm. The woman moved back a couple of times before she took two or three pictures.

"See if any of these work." She handed Alanza her phone.

As she clicked between them, Alanza smiled. "They're great. Thank you."

While she showed the photos to Malcolm, the other couple moved past them.

Alanza studied the nativity scene. "Look at how exquisite the carving is on baby Jesus in the manger." She leaned close then backed up a little. "And Mary and Joseph are so attentive to Him."

He joined her and put his arm around her again. "It looks almost like carved crystal."

"It makes me want to sing 'Away in a Manger.'"

"So, go ahead." He smiled.

She hesitated for a moment. "Will you sing, too? Kind of like we're caroling?"

How could he deny her something so simple that would make her happy? "Okay."

While they stood there singing, several other groups of people came through the freezing room. One even stayed to sing along with them. When they finished, Malcolm and Alanza moved on.

After a few steps, she stopped and looked at him. "That almost felt like a worship service, didn't it?"

He nodded in agreement.

WHEN THEY EXITED the display and took off the ICE! polar coats, Alanza led the way across the hallway where a hot chocolate stand was set up. "A smart place for this. I'm sure everyone comes out as cold as I am."

Malcolm bought large cups for both of them. They wandered down the hallway into an area with tables and chairs. They sat near the windows where the late afternoon sun streamed through, bathing them in warmth.

Alanza took a sip. The yummy liquid was really hot. Like, burn your mouth hot. So she cupped her hands around the container, trying to get her fingers to thaw out. Even though she had worn gloves in the exhibit, they hadn't kept her hands warm enough.

She set her cup down, and he reached across the table and clasped one of her hands in his. How could he be warm already? But she welcomed it.

"I'm glad you brought me out here, Malcolm. And I loved that the tour ended with a nativity scene to remind people of the true meaning of Christmas."

So many Christmas decorations and displays don't have any connection to what Christmas is truly about. Alanza wished there were more like this one, where the nativity scene had a prominent place.

"I almost asked you if you wanted to go down one of the ice slides, but you were shivering so much, I knew the answer before I could ask you." He took a large gulp of his cocoa.

Surely it hadn't cooled down that much. She took a small sip again. Still too hot to drink. "You must be used to drinking really hot liquids." She studied him across the top of her cup.

He grinned at her and took another swig. "Just right. I do like my coffee hot. If it's lukewarm, why bother drinking it? I think a drink should be either really hot or really cold. Not tepid like the church in Laodicea in the book of Revelation. I like icy cold sweet tea, even in the wintertime." He grinned. "And of course a nice cold Dr Pepper."

Alanza gave him an indulgent smile. "I don't usually drink lukewarm coffee or cocoa, but I also don't want to burn my tongue." She took another sip. Thankfully, it was finally cooling off.

His face softened, and he looked at her with a kind of spark in his eyes. "You are so radiant, sitting here in the sunlight. I could look at you all day and never get tired of it."

Flabbergasted, she didn't know what to say. After a few moments of silence, she whispered, "Thank you." She wanted to compliment him, but the words wouldn't come. So she concentrated on her hot chocolate, trying to cover her embarrassment.

For a while, they watched the people passing by, and she made up little stories about what was going on with each group.

"Are you a writer?" Malcolm leaned his forearms on the edge of the table, turned up his cup, and drained it.

She shook her head. "Sometimes, I do write a little bit. And of course, I journal when I study the Bible. Why do you ask?"

"Your insights about people remind me of my older sister's best friend. She's an author and writes Christian novels. Have you ever thought about doing something like that?" He stared at her as if she were some kind of exotic creature.

She wasn't sure how much to tell him. She once started to share her dream of being a writer with a guy she dated in college and he mocked her. So she'd never mentioned it again. "Actually, I do have stories that go over and over in my head. But I haven't had time to pursue anything like that." She couldn't tell him about her idea for a novel. *Not yet. Maybe never.*

"What was your major in college?" He clasped his hands as he continued to study her.

"Business. To help my parents with the restaurant. We've used many of the things I learned to make it more successful." She glanced down at her cup and took another drink. "But I did minor in creative writing. Maybe someday, I'll try to write a book."

"You know, you amaze me. You're an artist, you know about business, and you're a great storyteller."

She basked in his praise. No other man ever encouraged her the way Malcolm did. She finished her drink, got up, and took their empty cups to the trash can beside the wall.

He followed her. "Let's check out some of the other things until the sun goes down."

Taking her hand, he walked beside her as they headed down a long hallway toward the atrium. When they reached one side, he led her into another wide corridor that went around the atrium where they had a good view of all the decorations.

"There are some stores along this hallway." He stopped in front of one.

They wandered through the shelves of souvenirs of Texas and the Dallas-Fort Worth Metroplex and browsed a variety of clothing, most with logos or slogans on them.

"I can see why travelers would like to shop here. It appears to have almost everything a person might have forgotten to pack." Alanza turned to look at Malcolm. He didn't seem to be enjoying all of the crowded merchandise, so she took his hand and led him out the door.

They continued by a coffee shop to an area with some upscale shops. One had women's clothing with unique styles that appealed to her. "I'd like to see if there's anything in here I really want."

"Go ahead." He glanced around. "I'll just stay out here and see if there's any other shop we might want to visit."

She eagerly plunged into the displays. Soon she had four different, very unusual tops to take to the fitting room. After trying on each one, she bought them all. It wasn't often she found this many things at once that she really liked and she hadn't gone shopping just for herself in quite a while. When she finished paying, she went to the entrance.

Malcolm leaned against the wall beside the manne-quin-filled windows. He stepped forward to meet her. "I see you found some things you like."

"Yes." She slipped the two bags on one arm and slid her hand into his.

"Now we need to see the atrium with all the lights." He led the way.

When they stepped inside, she couldn't keep from oooing and ahhhing. Long strings of tiny lights hung from the dome, looking like shimmering rain. Everywhere they looked, all kinds of Christmas decorations clustered around them. A train that small children could ride chugged around the perimeter.

They walked up and down the many walkways through the atrium, enjoying everything. Finally, Malcolm led her to the top of the knoll in the middle. Even though many other people walked around, the two park benches on the knoll were empty. They sat down side by side.

"You were right." She squeezed his hand. "I love it here. Thank you for bringing me."

"My pleasure."

He reached into his coat pocket and pulled out a box. "I didn't have time to get this wrapped. I just found it while you were shopping." He held it out toward her.

She could see a jewelry store's name embossed in gold on the top. "It's not Christmas yet."

"I know. I'm just your friend who found something he wanted to give you as a gift today… with no strings attached."

The iPad had been too much. He shouldn't have bought her anything else. Still, she was curious. She accepted the box and opened it. Nestled in soft, white cotton was a black plastic card with earrings attached. Gold earrings in the shape of a snow-flake, studded with pearls.

"I couldn't pass them up. They match the pretty brooch you wore to church today. I wanted you to have them.

"Thank you. They're beautiful." They really were. "But you have to stop giving me a present every day. It's too much." *Not to mention all the money he has spent taking me out to eat!*

In response, all he did was smile.

9

Monday – Nine Days Before Christmas

fter the wonderful weekend, Alanza wasn't eager to go back to work. Malcolm wasn't far from her thoughts. His question hung between them like a pendulum that had stopped swinging. *Is there anything about me you wouldn't want in a husband?*

Nothing that she knew of. He was everything she wanted. *But things are moving too fast. I never even laid eyes on him until three weeks ago. Seeing him eat at the restaurant a few times, then having three dates. That's not enough to hang a marriage on.*

Yes, she felt more comfortable with him than she ever had with any other man, and shared things with him she'd never told anyone. Not even her family. Her parents didn't know she minored in creative writing. They were more interested in how her business major could help the restaurant.

Alanza arrived at Cantalamessa's just before she needed to start work, but she really wanted to talk to her parents about the weekend. Maybe they'd have time when her shift was over.

Before that, she had Malcolm's lunch break to look forward to. If her parents saw them together, they might suspect some of what took place. Not that anything untoward had happened.

When she went to the back room to clock in, her cell phone rang. She pulled it from her pocket. Malcolm. Had he been thinking about her as much as she'd been thinking about him?

"Hello?" She used her most cheerful voice, glad no one was nearby.

"Hi, Alanza." His voice wasn't as upbeat. "I have some bad news."

That didn't sound good. "What kind of news?"

"Everything is crazy here at work. I'm not going to make it to lunch and I might be working late. This project is taking more time than I thought it would."

He did sound as if he were sorry.

And so was she. "I'll miss seeing you."

"And I'll miss you. Maybe I can come over when I get off... if that's all right with you." He sounded hopeful.

Good. He wants to see me. "Sure, if it's not too late."

"I'll try to make sure it isn't. Gotta go."

After she said a quick goodbye, the click of him ending the call sounded loud on her phone. She turned around as she slipped it into her pocket.

Mamma stood just inside the swinging doors, staring at her. "Is everything all right?"

Now wasn't the time to get into the conversation about Malcolm. "Yes, Mamma. I'll go unlock the front door now."

The day crept along like a sloth climbing a tree branch. When the lunch crowd thinned, she felt as if it should be the dinner crowd leaving. Way past the time she should get off.

"Is something the matter, Alanza?" How long had Mamma been standing right beside her? Watching her?

"Why do you think something's wrong?" She tried for a bright smile but wasn't sure she succeeded.

"You've been in a daze today. No bright smiles and greetings for the customers." Mamma frowned. "Some of the regulars noticed, too."

"I'm sorry." She turned and waited on another departing diner, careful to use her usual banter and smile.

"That's better." Mother patted her shoulder. "If something's bothering you, I'm right here if you want to talk about it."

That's the invite I need. "I *would* like to talk to you and Poppa when my shift is over, if you have time."

"I'm sure we can make time for our darling girl." Her mother's voice took on a soft, loving tone.

Alanza's break occurred after most of the lunch crowd left. She went back to the kitchen to see if any of the day's pasta special was left. It was one of her favorites, her Uncle Stefano's own recipe. It consisted of a hearty meat sauce interspersed with layers of spaghetti and mozzarella, ricotta, Asiago, and provolone cheese.

Her uncle looked up as she walked in. "Alanza, I saved you a helping of spaghetti lasagna. I'll toast you some garlic bread, too."

"Thank you! You're always so good to me." She gave him a hug, then went to the salad station. "I'll make my own salad while the bread heats."

Just as she drizzled dressing on the salad, her mother entered the kitchen. She asked Stefano to heat up some of the lunch special for her. Then she made a salad for herself and joined her daughter.

"Your father had to meet with one of the vendors. He probably won't be back before you get off work. Let's eat in the office so we can visit in private."

Her mother didn't mean it like an order, but that's how it sounded to Alanza. Probably best to get it over with now. Then the events wouldn't be weighing down her thoughts like an anchor.

Besides the desk and file cabinets, a small table with two chairs provided a welcome place where they could eat away from the hustle and bustle of the kitchen. She grabbed a soft drink from the small refrigerator in one corner. Her father thought sodas tasted best coming from glass bottles, and Alanza agreed with him. After they both set their plates on the table, she went back to the kitchen to get two glasses of ice, leaving her mother to open the drinks.

They sat and bowed their heads while her mother said the blessing over their food.

"So why didn't we see you over the weekend?"

Alanza had just taken her first bite when the questions started.

"Even when you're off Saturday and Sunday, you either drop by the restaurant or we see you in church."

Alanza put down her fork. "I'm sure Poppa told you I had a date Friday night."

Mamma nodded. "I understand it was with that nice man who's recently started coming here. I haven't met him. What's his name?"

"Malcolm MacGregor." She took another bite of her pasta.

"A nice Scottish name. And easy on the eyes, I must say."

Alanza's lips turned up in a slight smile. She'd never heard her mother say anything like that about any man besides Poppa. "Yes, very easy." She had to corral a giggle that tried to escape.

"Where did you go?" Mamma studied her intently.

"He took me out to dinner on Friday night." She sipped her Dr Pepper. "At a bistro in a residential neighborhood in Bedford. I'm not sure the name of it. It's in a historic house that's more like an estate, and you have to know about it to find it. But the food was excellent."

"I've heard about that place, but your Poppa and I haven't tried to find it."

"You should go. Malcolm can tell you how to get there."

Her mother put her fork on the edge of her plate. "I'm assuming you were with Mr. MacGregor some more over the weekend?"

Alanza couldn't contain the smile that spread across her face. "Yes."

"So tell me." Mamma must be trying to analyze her responses to Malcolm.

"He took me to breakfast on Saturday." Alanza didn't want to tell Mamma any more information than necessary.

Her mother laughed. "Don't you usually sleep late on your Saturdays off?"

"Yes. He called me early and woke me up. We went to the Oldwest Café in Euless."

"Sounds interesting." Mamma started eating again.

Oh, well, I might as well tell her. So Alanza talked about where they went on Saturday and Sunday, what they did. But she didn't mention the gifts. She was still trying to figure out what she should do about them.

"That was quite a lot of time you spent together."

Alanza couldn't tell if her mother was upset or not.

"But it's not enough to explain how you're acting today. What brought that on?"

She had thought she was ready to talk to her parents about all of this, but now she realized, she wasn't. How could she make her mother understand her feelings? She really liked Malcolm a lot, but he was moving way too fast. How could she express this without her mother getting the wrong impression about him?

She heaved a deep sigh. "He asked me to tell him if there was anything about him that I wouldn't want in a husband. He's ready to settle down."

Mamma's eyes widened. "Alanza, you hardly know the man. How could you answer that question? It might be a major red flag. What did you say?"

"Nothing."

"Nothing? Why not?"

Alanza took another bite and chewed it slowly, trying to decide how much to tell her. "I know I don't know him well enough to say. But everything I *do* know about him is good. He's kind, gentle, has the best manners... The only thing is, he's moving too fast."

"Too fast? Alanza, has he tried to push you into... into bed?" Mamma sounded almost hysterical.

"No! He's a Christian. When we were at church, he really got into the worship and he listened intently to every word the preacher said and we even talked about it afterward. I *am* twenty-four after all, Mamma, and sometimes guys do try to move

too fast physically. But he doesn't do any of that. And he goes to the same church we do, just at the other campus."

Her mother studied her. "I just want you to be careful."

"I am, Mamma. I'm older than you were when you met Poppa, and I've never given you any reason not to trust me. This sounds like a serious case of 'do as I say, not as I do.' You only spent one week getting to know Poppa before he came back to the U.S. And when he went back to Brazil one month later, it was for your wedding."

Mother dropped her fork on her plate, leaving an uneaten bite, got up, and left without asking any more questions or saying another word. The atmosphere in the office was heavy with what was left unsaid.

As she watched her mother walk out of the office, Alanza rubbed her eyes, wishing she'd thought before she spoke. She could have phrased it better. Mamma didn't deserve what she said, even if she did feel that way.

MALCOLM RUBBED HIS hand on the back of his neck. It had been a killer of a day, but he finished everything he needed to and was able to leave work on time. He'd go home, take a shower, put on fresh clothes, and then call Alanza. After spending part or most of the last three days with her, he yearned to see her again. Just thinking about it perked him up.

He pulled into his space in the covered parking area at the apartment. Slinging his jacket over his shoulder, he grabbed his briefcase and headed inside.

"Malcolm, so glad to see you." His father's voice startled him.

He looked up to find both his father and his grandmother sitting in the living room of the apartment. "How did *you* get in here?" He instantly regretted it. He didn't mean to sound so brusque.

His father stood. "Eric let us in."

Confused, Malcolm grimaced. "Eric doesn't get home until after I do."

"He got off early today and called us. He said we needed to talk to you about something."

"What are you talking about?" He asked the question, knowing that Eric probably stuck his nose in where it didn't belong. If he did, it wouldn't be the first time.

"Son, why didn't you tell us about your promotion?"

"And about your move to Australia?" Hurt infused Nanna's tone.

"And about this woman you're involved with?" His father sounded angry, like Malcolm was still a teenager.

Because he was so tired, he couldn't keep his temper from flaring up. "He had no right to tell you any of that!"

Nanna shrank back into her chair, and he wished he hadn't lashed out.

"I'm sorry." He shook his head, rueful. "I planned to tell you about it when I felt it was time. Especially with another person involved."

His father thrust his hands into the front pockets of his slacks. "Just how involved are you with this person?"

"*Faither...*" Frustrated, Malcolm started to pace. "I'm not a teenager. I'm twenty-six years old. And I know how to deal with my business and personal life."

He regretted the words as soon as they left his mouth. Hurt flickered in his father's eyes.

Malcolm counted to ten in his mind and took a few deep breaths. "I'm sorry. I didn't mean to be so harsh, but this was all such a surprise to me, too. Australia. This woman..."

His grandmother's smile trembled. "It was quite a shock for us, too."

"I had planned to tell everyone soon, but I had promised Arabella she'd be the first person I told about the woman when I was ready because..."

"We know about the tartan bow she made for you." His father's tone still sounded censuring. "Giving a woman a tartan is tantamount to asking her to marry you. Does this woman understand that?"

"I did ask her to tell me if there was anything about me she wouldn't want in a husband."

Nanna leaned forward again. "And what did she say?"

"Nothing." He deflated like a balloon. "I told her that if she decided there wasn't anything, she could wear the bow to let me know." As he spoke the words out loud, the whole idea sounded stupid.

Now it was his father's turn to pace. "Whatever made you think she might want to marry you? Does she know how wealthy we are?"

Really, Faither? You think I would fall for a gold digger? "Her family is well-off on their own. They own Cantalamessa's Gourmet Pizzas and More on Highway 10."

Malcolm's father stopped right in front of him. "I've eaten there with some of my golf partners. It's a nice place. Always busy."

"To answer your other question, *Faither*, I prayed about starting a relationship with her. I spent most of one night seeking the Lord. He revealed to me that she's the woman he created to be my wife." There, he'd said it out loud to someone else. Someone who knew the Lord as well as he did.

Maxwell MacGregor rubbed his chin, then sat back down.

Malcolm's grandmother smiled at him and turned toward his father. "This sounds a lot like what happened with Dan and Rose Baker. You remember. They told us about how God placed in Dan's heart a calling to be a missionary in Mexico and plant churches. When he reached the border, he stopped and stayed a while. He understood he shouldn't go into Mexico as a single man, so he sought God about it. Soon God sent Rose, who was a fairly new Christian, to the border town where he was. When she walked in, God revealed to him that she was to be his wife. If God could do it back then, he can speak to our boy and tell him who He prepared to be his wife."

His father nodded. "You're right. It's possible."

Malcolm closed his eyes as Nanna's words fell around him like a refreshing rain. He sat beside her on the sofa and hugged her.

AFTER THEY LEFT, he called Alanza. "I was able to get away sooner than I thought. I need to clean up and change clothes. How about I come in an hour or so?"

"Sure. Have you eaten?" The sound of her voice was like music to his ears.

"Not yet. Do you want to go out somewhere?" He was tired, but he'd be glad to do whatever she wanted.

"No. Uncle Stefano fixed one of my favorite pastas today. I brought enough home to share with you. We can eat here, if that's all right with you. And I'll make salads for us."

"That's fine with me. Thanks, Alanza." Actually, more than fine. It sounded like heaven to him right then.

As they hung up, his doorbell rang. He opened the door to a FedEx driver.

"Here's a package for Malcolm MacGregor. You need to sign here."

After he signed for it, he brought the package in and opened it. *Good.* Something he'd ordered for Alanza. He'd take it over to her tonight.

He hurried through his shower and dressed casually. Arriving at her apartment in less than an hour, Malcolm hoped he wasn't too early. He really wanted to see her. He hoped she'd be wearing the tartan bow. If she did, he'd sweep her into his arms, and they'd share their first kiss.

Grabbing the box, he hurried up her steps. She answered immediately when he rang the bell. He glanced at her hair... no bow. He had to wait a little longer for his answer, whether he wanted to or not.

She led the way to the kitchen. The table was set, and the aroma of the pasta dish permeated the room.

"Smells good in here—and I'm hungry." He smiled at her. "I brought you something. Maybe we can have it for dessert."

"I can't wait to open it." She set the fairly large box on the counter. There was a medium-sized Styrofoam container inside. He lifted it out for her. She opened it. "What are these?"

"On our first date, you told me how much you like chocolate-covered cherries. When my sister's friend, the novelist, signed with a new publisher, they welcomed her to the company by sending her these. She brought some over to the house. They are gourmet chocolate-covered cherries from an online company. See, there are dark chocolate ones, milk chocolate ones, and even white chocolate. Each one is hand dipped."

She gazed into his eyes. "Do we have to wait until dessert to try one?"

"They're yours. You can do whatever you want with them."

She picked up a dark chocolate one and savored it by making two bites out of it.

"Now you have one." She took another and held it right in front of his lips.

He was tempted to kiss her fingers as he took the sweet, but no. *I can't push her. She needs to believe God has chosen me for her and her for me.* He opened his mouth and let her slip it in. He'd almost forgotten how good they were.

She dished out their food and set it on the table. "Let's eat, then I'll tell you about my day and you can tell me about yours."

Doing normal things was just what he needed right now. How soon would he need to tell her everything?

10

Tuesday – Eight Days Before Christmas

Malcolm awoke in a bad mood.

He was glad he'd been able to spend more special time with Alanza last night. The food was delicious and the dessert fun. They had shared anecdotes about things that happened to them when they were children. Most of the stories made them laugh, which helped him relax. Being with Alanza calmed him. God knew what He was doing when He created them to be together.

She told him about her lunch with her mother. That didn't bode well for his first meeting with Jacolin Cantalamessa. He wanted to set up a time right away to have a talk with both of Alanza's parents. They needed to know his intentions for their daughter were honorable. The sooner he met with them, the better.

One thing in his life was very wrong. Eric Summerfield. *What the heck was he thinking? How am I supposed to deal with his butting his nose into my business like that?*

They were both twenty-six. Malcolm was sure Eric wouldn't ever want him to interfere with anything in his life the way Eric had in Malcolm's. He actually wanted to punch Eric's lights out. For a moment, he wished they were still boys, when they took care of their disagreements with both fists flying. They always forgave each other when it was all over. Malcolm didn't know how soon he could forgive Eric this time.

He'd waited up quite a while for Eric to come home last night, but his roommate was a no-show. Malcolm headed toward the other bedroom. He slowly opened the door, hoping to find Eric asleep. But the bed hadn't been slept in. *There's always tonight. I'll talk to him when he comes home tonight.* Unless Eric was deliberately staying away because he knew how ticked off Malcolm was. *Wonder how long it'll take him to come home.*

Malcolm knew he shouldn't be this angry with Eric, but calling Malcolm's family and spilling the beans like that was unbelievable. Since then, Malcolm had been ignoring the still small voice whispering in his mind and heart. *The Bible says we should forgive each other and not hold grudges.* Malcolm was sure that giving Eric the pounding he deserved would be considered a sin. Someone who didn't really know the Lord the way he did probably wouldn't think so though.

Maybe giving Eric a good talking to, reminding him of the boundary he had crossed, would work. No friend should cross the line like that. But since Eric had drifted so far from his Christian roots, fighting him would only push him farther from the God who loved them both.

After he finished getting ready for work, he called Mr. Cantalamessa. They worked out a time for Malcolm to come

by before the dinner rush. He hoped the Cantalamessas would understand what was going on. He wouldn't be able to tell them the reasons behind his rush because he hadn't shared that information with Alanza yet. He was waiting for her to get comfortable enough with their relationship that she could understand. Last night, they had come quite a way down that road… but she hadn't worn the bow yet.

Soon after he arrived at work, his cell phone rang. *Grandmother.* The only way to find out what she wanted was to take the call, so he closed his office door.

"Nanna, you don't usually call me at work. Is everything okay?" He stared out the window, watching rain run down the glass, making downtown Fort Worth look like an Impressionist painting.

"Nothing's wrong, Malcolm. I just wanted to ask you a question." He heard joy in her voice.

"Yes, Nanna, what is it?" He hoped she wouldn't start a long explanation of something. He really didn't have a lot of time to talk.

"I want to fix dinner for you and Alanza. It's time we met her. It'll only be your father, Arabella, the two of you, and me. We can have a family dinner closer to Christmas so everyone else can meet her. Do you think you can come tonight?"

The hopefulness in her voice tugged at his heartstrings. Just then, the quick winter shower moved away, and the sun came out from behind the clouds. He wouldn't rain on his grandmother's plans. "I'll call her and see if we can work that out."

After telling Nanna goodbye, he clicked the button to call Alanza's cell. He'd told her last night about his maternal grandmother coming to stay with his family when his mother died. She'd been the one who kept the family together through all the

grieving process. And *Faither* had asked her to live with them. She had been lonely and gladly anchored the family in their home.

"This is Alanza. I'm busy working right now. Leave a message and I'll call you soon."

Of course, if she was working, she wouldn't answer the phone. He left her a message about the invitation to dinner. He hoped she heard it in time for him to let Nanna know if they were coming tonight. She would want to start meal preparations early in the day.

His day and evening were now full. He would need to finish quite a few things before he went to Cantalamessa's for the meeting with Alanza's parents. That way, he and Alanza would have plenty of time to change clothes and get to his father's house before dinner.

Mid-morning, his ringtone for Alanza pealed from his phone. He was glad he was in his own office and not in a meeting in the conference room.

"Hello, beautiful."

"Malcolm, what if someone else was using my phone? Like Ignazio, for instance? Ooo, do you think he's beautiful?" They burst out laughing at the same time. "So, why did you call me?"

Evidently, she didn't listen to his message. His sister was like that, too. She'd look to see who called then call them back. Alanza sounded in a good mood this morning. He hoped it was because of the time they spent together last night.

"My grandmother invited us over for dinner tonight. She wants to meet you. My father and Bella are eager to meet you, too. It will just be the five of us." *And I want to spend another evening with you.*

"That sounds wonderful. What time will you pick me up?"

He could hear her smile in her voice. "Would six be too early?"

"No. I get off at three, and that will give me time to change and get ready. So how should I dress?"

She must think his family dressed formally for dinner. "Nice casual would be fine. See you at six."

ALANZA'S FATHER HAD told him they could meet at four. He hurried to finish up some work so he could leave downtown Fort Worth by three-thirty and miss the rush hour traffic.

The restaurant's parking lot was nearly empty when he pulled in. He'd never seen it like this, but then again, it was way too late for lunch and a little too early for dinner. The staff was probably busy getting ready for the evening crowd.

The dining room was empty, except for Alanza's parents, sitting at a table halfway down one side, by the windows, with sunshine streaming in. Malcolm headed toward them.

As he approached, Alanza's father stood. "Welcome, Malcolm. I don't believe you've met my wife yet. Dear, this is Malcolm MacGregor. And this is my wife, Jacolin."

Malcolm now knew where Alanza got her good looks. "I'm so pleased to meet you, Mrs. Cantalamessa. Alanza has told me so much about you."

The woman stood, tall like Alanza and slim. Actually, she looked a lot like her daughter. Malcolm once read a travel story that said Brazilian women "are the complete embodiment of female sexuality." Meeting Alanza's mother, he could see why.

"And I've heard a lot about you, Malcolm." She held out one hand for him.

He shook it and smiled. "I hope it was all good." Although she seemed to welcome him, he also sensed her holding back. Guarded.

"Have a seat." Alanza's father indicated he should sit across from them. "I ordered you a Dr Pepper. That is your drink of choice, isn't it?"

"Yes, sir."

Jacolin Cantalamessa had the same eyes and hair that her daughter did, but she wore her hair in an elegant figure-eight chignon resting on the back of her neck.

Ignazio came over with a Dr Pepper and two coffees. Malcolm smiled at him. "Thank you, Ignazio."

The waiter nodded and retreated.

Alessandro took a sip of coffee and let out a satisfied sigh. "So what did you want to talk to us about, Malcolm?"

"Alanza, sir." He cleared his throat. Why did he always get nervous when things were so important?

Alessandro leaned his forearms on the table and clasped his hands. "When you asked if you could ask our daughter out for a date, I remember you mentioning marriage. I thought your relationship would move slow and easy. But you've spent a lot of time with her during the last four days. That seems a little excessive to her mother and me."

Malcolm wanted to handle this delicately, but he also wanted to be honest with them. "I was glad to learn that your family attends the same church I do. Just a different campus."

"Yes, that's true." He glanced at his wife. She nodded. "We came from a Catholic background. We don't live near a Catholic church, so we wanted to find somewhere else to worship. We visited a lot of churches, but none of them seemed to fit. When Way of Life Church opened, we decided to give it a try. For some reason, it felt like home to us."

Malcolm relaxed. He was comfortable talking about things like this. "My family chose Way of Life for much the same reason you did. My ancestors brought the Church of Scotland with them when they immigrated to the U.S. in the 1700s and settled in the mountains of North Carolina. But it was just conducted by clan leaders, since no clergymen came. As the clans scattered across the states, some places didn't have kirks, so many members of my clan have integrated into other churches."

Alessandro and Jacolin shared a glance, seeming to communicate without saying a word. Couples are like that when their marriage is strong, Malcolm realized. His parents were like that before his mother died.

"So what does all this have to do with you and our daughter?" Jacolin's voice had the same musical cadence and flow as Alanza's did.

"A lot of people might not understand what I want to tell you, but I'm sure you will since you've been hearing the sermons at Way of Life."

That caught their attention. Both leaned forward and trained their eyes on him.

"When I started coming here, Alanza quickened something in my heart. I've been praying for some time about who God

wants me to marry. Since college, I've not dated casually. I haven't wanted to give any woman expectations I can't fulfill. So I've gone out with groups of people instead."

Jacolin's eyes widened, and she reached for Alessandro's hand.

Malcolm cleared his throat. "After coming here several times, I spent most of one night seeking the Lord. I asked Him to take away my fascination with Alanza if she wasn't the one I was to marry. He didn't. Instead, He assured me that He had created her to be my wife. I'm twenty-six and she's twenty-four. I'm courting her with marriage in mind... as I told you, Mr. Cantalamessa, when I asked if I could ask her for a date. And I hope we won't have to wait a long time before we can get married."

Alessandro just studied Malcolm's face for a few moments. "Interesting," he said finally, slowly. "Maybe *we* should pray about whether we should approve."

"Of course." This wasn't the response Malcolm expected, but it was actually a good one. He knew what God had told him. The Lord could confirm to Alanza's parents what He told Malcolm. He prayed they would hear from Him.

ALANZA DIDN'T KNOW what Malcolm's family would consider "nice casual." Several outfits she'd chosen then discarded were

piled on her bed. Nothing appealed to her. She kept going far-ther and farther into the walk-in closet, checking each garment then going past it. Finally, she reached an area with clothing she hadn't worn in quite a while.

A pair of black woolen slacks looked brand new. *Perfect!* She took them out and laid them across a different part of her bed. Another cold front had come through. She needed something warm to wear. She found a long-sleeve, forest green, crushed velour shirt. *Yes! You were hiding back there all this time?* She laughed to herself. She had purchased that shirt last year and forgot about it. After she dressed and fixed her hair and makeup, she took a look in the full-length mirror on her closet door. What should she use to accessorize?

She glanced at her jewelry armoire. *Silly! You know what jewelry you must wear!* She got out the pearl-studded snowflake brooch and the matching earrings from Malcolm. She had just finished putting in the second earring when the doorbell chimed.

I wonder if I can get the doorbell to play a Christmas carol. Hmmm... Maybe she'd do that when she got home tonight.

Malcolm looked wonderful as always. *Beefy male model hot.*

"Right on time." She held the door open for him.

He entered and looked her over appreciatively, ending with her hair. When his gaze traveled there, disappointment flitted briefly in his eyes, but he quickly masked it.

"I could hardly wait to see you again." He took her hands in his and rested them on his chest. "Every moment I spend away from you feels like a day."

"I know." She trembled, wishing they were in a place in their relationship where he would kiss her. She knew that wouldn't happen until she wore the tartan bow.

He unbuttoned his winter coat and left the front open while he helped her into her long coat. His family might think they worked together to coordinate their clothing choices. He wore a forest green pullover sweater, white and green pin-striped shirt, and black pants.

Alanza loved the feel of his hands on her shoulders as he helped to straighten her coat. She turned around to face him. "Wow, I see you got the memo." They laughed. *That's it. Joke. Stay calm.* She didn't want his family to get the wrong impression about her.

They talked easily about their day as he drove toward his family's home. She was surprised when he told her about meeting with her parents. But now wasn't the time to ask what happened. She would on the way home.

She glanced out the window and realized they were driving through Southlake on 114. He took the Trophy Club exit and entered a gated community. When they were through the gate, she didn't see more than a couple of houses, set far back from the street. Huge houses. Mansions really. Did his family own a mansion? That might affect whether they accepted her... or not.

Malcolm turned on to a long driveway that wound around a large yard before she could see the three-story house. He pulled under a covered archway where the upper stories connected to the three-car garage.

While he walked around to open her door, the side door to the house opened and slammed shut. A young woman with bright red, corkscrew curls rioting in the wind rushed toward him. "Mal! So glad y'all finally got here."

"Nanna said we'd eat at seven. We're still early."

This must be Bella. Alanza hoped she'd pass muster with his sister. If she didn't, things might get a little uncomfortable.

"And who have you brought home with you?" The girl's gaze roved all over Alanza. "Come in. I want to know all about you."

Then she grabbed Alanza and hugged her—and something wonderful filled her heart.

Malcolm stood beside the two of them. "Alanza, this is my younger sister, Bella." He turned toward his sister. "And this is who you made the tartan bow for, Alanza Cantalamessa."

Malcolm's sister led the way through a wide hallway. Through one large archway, Alanza spotted a magnificent kitchen, with marble countertops, glass doors on an oversized refrigerator, and other great features. Actually, everything in this house was fantastic.

What if they don't think I'm good enough for Malcolm?

11

Alanza followed as Bella led her through the front foyer. It reminded her of the rotunda of the capital building in Washington, D.C.—much smaller, of course, but still large for a home. Two staircases connected with a balcony on the second floor, forming a horseshoe shape.

Bella took her coat and hung it in a closet under one of the staircases. "You can come to my room to freshen up. Nanna said the meal will be served at seven and it's only six-thirty."

She had a hard time keeping up with Bella because she was taking in all of the beautiful furniture and decorative items. She felt almost as if she were in a museum. Antiques and modern art blended to make a pleasing tableau in every room they passed.

"I love all the paintings." Alanza had studied Art Appreciation in college and recognized the work of several artists.

"You should see the ones in the third-floor gallery. Scottish ancestors for generations. Some of the older ones look fierce. They used to scare me when I was little. I wouldn't go to the gallery without my nanny. I believed she could protect me."

A nanny? Alanza felt out of her league.

Bella's "room" was a suite with a bathroom, sitting area, and bedroom. "Come in. There's plenty of room for both of us to get ready."

"Do you still live here with your father and grandmother?"

"Only on holidays and in the summertime. I'm a junior at UT Austin. When school is in session, I share an apartment with two other girls. We've been friends since kindergarten."

Alanza was impressed. UT Austin was a fairly recent addition to the list of Ivy League schools. The only one in Texas. "What are you majoring in?" She sat on one of the cozy chairs in Bella's bedroom.

Bella sat on the edge of her king-sized bed. "I attend the College of Fine Arts. I'd like to be a librarian at a large library… or own an art gallery."

Lofty goals. Alanza realized she and Bella had a lot in common. She sat on the bed beside her. "My mother is a well-known artist. She's just got home from a one-woman show at a gallery in New York City. We often paint together."

"Really?" Bella was impressed. "Have you displayed any of *your* work in a gallery?"

"Not yet. But we worked together on the murals in our family restaurant."

"I get it now." Bella turned a bright smile toward her. "Cantalamessa? That's your last name? Your family owns the restaurant on Highway 10."

Alanza nodded.

"I *love* that place. My friends and I always stop in there when we're home from university. And now, you and I are almost sisters." She grinned.

Good Lord, what has Malcolm told them? That he wants to marry me? We need to have a long talk—tonight.

When Alanza stood, the tartan bow on top of Bella's chest of drawers caught her eye.

Bella noticed her glancing at it. "How did you like the one I made for you?"

"I love it." Alanza didn't know what else to say.

"Do you know what it means when a Scottish man gives a woman something with his tartan on it?" Bella didn't take her eyes off Alanza.

She nodded. "Yes. I'm pretty sure."

"Then why aren't you wearing it today? It would go so well with your outfit."

Alanza never felt so at a loss for words. She didn't want to tell Bella what was going on with Malcolm. It was no one's business except theirs. But she realized she had to make up her own mind about him very soon. *There is nothing about him that I wouldn't want in a husband. And I like being with him. Every moment has been wonderful.*

She had never believed in love at first sight, even knowing her own parents' story. But now, she wondered. Had she been wrong all these years?

"I'm saving it for a special occasion." Hopefully, that would stop the questions.

Bella led her into the bathroom, which was also a suite. A lavatory, dressing table with a bench, and the open door to a huge walk-in closet were in the dressing area. She couldn't imagine having so much room for herself. Half of her whole apartment would fit inside Bella's suite.

While Bella went into the closet, Alanza sat on the bench and studied herself in the mirror above the table. Her makeup looked fine, but she had to fix her hair. The wind had messed it up.

Among the bottles on Bella's dressing table was a bottle of Inis cologne. Alanza loved this Irish fragrance. A cousin gave her a small bottle after a trip to the British Isles.

She picked it up the bottle, took off the lid, and took a quick sniff. *Ah…* She loved the ocean-fresh fragrance with refreshing citrus and lily of the valley.

"You can try that if you want to." Bella suddenly appeared right behind her.

Startled, Alanza dropped the bottle of cologne. It fell against the edge of the marble top of the dressing table. A crack appeared in the bottle before it hit the floor and shattered.

Alanza wished she could also just disappear into the carpet. "I'm so sorry! I didn't mean to break it."

Bella smiled at her. "It's okay." She went into the bedroom and spoke into an intercom.

When she returned, she gave Alanza a hug. "The maid will be here in a bit to clean it up. Don't worry about it."

"But I know you can only get Inis in Ireland. My cousin gave me some a few years ago. I loved it but didn't have any way to get more."

Bella turned back toward the mirror. "I order it online. It's available here in the U.S."

"Of course." Alanza felt a little silly. "I'll order another bottle for you."

Bella laughed. "Nonsense. I always have a couple of bottles on hand. Maybe I'll order a bottle for *you*."

"That would be wonderful. Thank you." Alanza relaxed and reapplied her lipstick.

"If you're ready, you can go ahead back downstairs. I'll be down soon. Just go to the central hallway and follow the voices. You'll find everyone in the parlor."

When Alanza walked into the room, everyone stopped talking. All eyes were on her, making her uncomfortable. *Were they talking about me?* Malcolm's father and grandmother were sitting close together. When they looked at her, was there guilt in their expressions? So her fears were right. They didn't want her to be part of their family. That thought cut straight to her heart.

Malcolm quickly rose from his seat. "Come on in, Alanza. I want you to meet my father and grandmother." He stopped beside her and put his arm around the back of her waist.

During the introductions, she studied his father, Maxwell MacGregor, and his grandmother, Grace Campbell. She didn't see any indication that either of them didn't like her. *Maybe I was wrong. Maybe they were just having a family conversation.*

Malcolm's grandmother stood and lived up to her name. She wore her snow-white hair braided and wound around her head, like a coronet. It gave her a regal bearing. She gave Alanza a sweet smile. "I believe cook has everything ready to serve."

Maxwell stood as well. "Where's Bella?"

"I'm here." Bella stood in the open doorway with one hand behind her back. "Y'all go on in. I need a word with Malcolm before we join you."

What's that all about?

Maxwell took Alanza's arm and led her to the formal dining room. A festive holiday runner covered a long table, with Christmas flowers and decorations set at even intervals. She mentally counted the chairs. Thirty. Five places were set at one end and Maxwell pulled out a chair for her to sit on his right.

Soon Malcolm joined them, taking the empty place beside her.

He leaned toward her. "Sorry, Bella needed to tell me something."

Evidently something they didn't want me to hear. Again, she felt out of place.

The meal was accompanied with many friendly questions and answers, family stories, and a lot of laughter. Gradually, she felt accepted. Even loved.

Why did she have expectations of rejection earlier? She'd never experienced that before. *Not because of their wealth, surely.* Things like that weren't really important to her... at least she didn't think they were.

All too soon, it seemed, the household staff served a fabulous Baked Alaska for dessert. After she savored her first bite, she gazed at Malcolm's grandmother. "This is delicious."

"We don't have it very often. Cook wanted to celebrate Malcolm bringing a young lady to meet the family. She's fond of him and this is one of his favorite desserts."

Alanza glanced at him, and a blush crept up his neck and into his cheeks. She hadn't seen many men blush like he did. *Maybe it has something to do with all that red hair.*

She turned back toward Mrs. Campbell. "Please tell the cook I thought it was amazing. And the pot roast and vegetables were delicious as well."

Bella laughed. "Cook did the dessert and salad, but you can thank Nanna for the roast. She wanted to prepare something for you herself."

Alanza gave Mrs. Campbell her most winsome smile. "Thank you so much for the lovely meal." Now she felt bad about her earlier misplaced feelings of rejection. They had spent over two hours together, eating and talking. And Malcolm's family all seemed to accept her.

Mrs. Campbell walked with Alanza as they left the dining room. "I'm so glad to get to know you, dear, but it's been a long day for me, so I'm going to say good evening. I hope you'll come again soon."

Alanza wanted to hug her but refrained. This time. If she and Malcolm grew closer, she would feel like she could.

Malcolm walked beside them. When they reached the foyer, Malcolm reached down to his grandmother and encased her in his strong arms. He dropped a kiss on the top of her head. "I love you, Nanna."

Seeing the way he treated his grandmother almost made Alanza cry. It was so loving. Another thing on the positive side of her list. And the negative side was still empty. Was there anything negative about him, and she just wasn't seeing it? She hoped not.

Bella and Mr. MacGregor had followed them into the foyer. They watched Nanna make her way up the stairs.

Malcolm turned to his father and gave him a sideways hug. "Thanks, Faither. It's been wonderful, but we've both had a long day and I should get Alanza home."

When he hugged Bella, it was with both arms.

MALCOLM WENT OUTSIDE to bring his car to the side door. Bella accompanied Alanza there. Malcolm was so glad his sister approved of her. That had been one hurdle he'd been dreading. But it went well as evidenced by what his sister gave him earlier.

On the way to Alanza's apartment, their conversation was all about the evening. She glowed while they were talking. Everything went better than he'd ever imagined. The only thing keeping him from telling her about Australia was the fact she hadn't worn the hair clip yet. Until she did, he wasn't really sure where he stood with her.

He felt a special connection between them, and he thought she did, too. *What is keeping her from wearing her tartan bow?*

She invited him in when they arrived at her apartment. "The wind was pretty cold. Would you like some hot chocolate? I want to try a different recipe for it."

"Sounds good to me." He hung their coats in the hall closet.

Alanza headed toward the kitchen, and he followed. She didn't look back at him, so he set the wrapped package on the seat of a chair at the table.

Tonight, she set a pan with chocolate milk on her stovetop. While it slowly heated, she shaved part of a German chocolate bar into the pan.

His mouth watered. This would be some really good cocoa. "Where did you get the recipe for this?" He went to stand beside her as she worked.

She glanced up at him and smiled. "I've been looking at different recipes on the Internet. I'm combining several of the ideas into my creation."

Oh, how he wanted to kiss those smiling lips! *Maybe now... or maybe wait until they tasted like chocolate.* He shook his head. He needed to banish thoughts like this from his mind until she wore the hair bow. Why had he put that condition on the gift? If he hadn't, maybe they'd be farther along in their relationship. He had to keep reminding himself they had only been seeing each other for five days. *Five days!* They had spent so much time together, it seemed like more... yet not enough. He didn't have a lot more time before he'd need an answer from her.

She dipped up a little of the chocolate and tasted it. "It's hot enough now."

After pouring it into two oversized mugs, she took a can of real whipped cream out of the fridge and squirted a sweet mountaintop into each cup. Once again, she started shaving the chocolate bar, this time over the waiting mugs. When she returned the can to the refrigerator, she brought out a jar of maraschino cherries and topped each foamy mound with two.

"Do you want to sit here at the table or in the living room?" She handed him a mug.

"Here's fine." That would work out well for what he had in mind.

She placed coasters on the table then set her own hot chocolate on one of them. He sat across from her, near the wrapped package. After sitting down, she picked a long-stemmed cherry

from the top. She popped the fruit in her mouth and pulled the stem off.

Holding it up, she gazed at him with a gleam in her eyes. "Do you know how to tie a knot in a cherry stem with your tongue?"

"Are you kidding? No one can do that."

She placed the stem in her mouth. He watched as she moved her mouth around, manipulating the stem. It only took about a minute before she pulled out the stem with a single knot in it. "Now see if you can do it." She picked one of the cherries from his hot chocolate and held it in front of his lips.

He bit off the cherry and ate it while she held the empty stem in front of him. Not one to back down from a challenge, he took the stem in his mouth. It felt strange, but as he started to manipulate it, he realized he probably *could* make a knot. He took longer than she had, but finally, he pulled out a perfect knot.

"See, I knew you could do it." She ate the other cherry from her mug then sipped the hot cocoa.

"You have some whipped cream…" He reached toward her nose, then pulled his hand back. "Actually, it's on the tip of your nose and your upper lip, kind of like a white moustache."

She wiped her nose and mouth with her napkin then got up to get a clean napkin and two spoons. "This will make it easier." She ate most of the whipped cream with her spoon, then stirred the rest into her cup.

After eating his second cherry, he did the same with his cocoa. Reaching down to the seat beside him, he brought out a wrapped package.

"Where did that come from?"

"You didn't think I'd let a day go by without giving you a gift, did you?"

Alanza sighed. "And I told you that you need to stop bringing me gifts every day. No one does that."

"I do." Spoken so strongly, his own words reminded him of wedding vows. Vows he wanted to pledge to her... and soon.

He scooted the package across the table closer to her. At first, she just stared at it. The paper was the design of his clan tartan. He'd hid it so quickly after he received it that he hadn't noticed.

"I didn't wrap it. Bella did." As soon as the words left his mouth, he realized that might not be the best thing to say.

"Oh, really?" Alanza pulled the package closer and carefully removed the ribbon and paper, revealing a box containing a bottle of Inis cologne. Her eyes teared up. "Why did Bella wrap this for you?"

"I actually had something else for you today, but she told me you liked this and I should give it to you."

She placed her hands over her face and began to really cry. He went around the table and pulled her up into his arms. She hid her face against his shoulder. He murmured, "It's okay" against her hair. *Why in the world is she crying? Because the gift is really from Bella?*

After a few minutes, she pulled away. "You don't understand. When I was in her room tonight before we went down to eat, I accidentally broke her bottle of Inis. She shouldn't have given me this. It might be all she had."

"No, it's not. I know for a fact that she orders several bottles at a time. Besides, I'm going to replace this one for her. In fact, I'll order two, to replace the one you accidentally broke, too."

He raised her chin gently with his right hand. "Why are you crying?"

"I totally misunderstood your family. After we arrived at your… mansion, I expected them to reject me." She wiped her cheeks with both palms.

"Why in the world would they do that?" He studied her beautiful face.

"I felt totally out of place." She took a step back. "I had no idea your family had so much money."

He felt like he'd been punched in the gut. "What difference does that make? Your family owns a thriving business. They're well off, too."

"They might think I'm a gold digger." She spat out the last two words. "Maybe Bella gave you that Inis to give to me because she feels sorry for me."

Ouch! That hurt. Malcolm took a deep breath. "It's nothing like that at all. You don't understand how we view our finances. We consider them a blessing from God—a blessing we can use to help those He tells us to bless. I don't want to go into every business venture that my family is involved in, but we're really not all about money."

He took her hand, led her into the living room, and pulled her down beside him. When she leaned against the back of the sofa, he put his arm around her shoulders.

"No one in my family would ever reject you or think of you as a gold digger. Bella gave me that cologne out of the love she feels for you."

12

Wednesday – Seven Days Before Christmas

Alanza woke up in a terrific mood. Last night with Malcolm was wonderful. They had a good talk—although not the conversation she planned for them to have. After all that happened at his father's house, she now realized Malcolm probably didn't tell his family they were getting married. Bella could've jumped to that conclusion because Alanza accepted the tartan bow. And maybe his sister was right. Time would tell.

Even after only five days together, she was considering wearing the bow. Today was another chance to get to know him a little more.

After showering and dressing for work, she went to the kitchen for breakfast. There was so much good food last night for dinner, maybe she should not eat too much this morning.

But the restaurant was usually busy Wednesdays. There would be a lot of work to do. Her mother always told her to start the day with a good breakfast. *What's in the fridge?* She settled for a couple slices of bacon, two eggs, and toast.

Fortified, she was ready to face the day. Just after she put the dishes in the dishwasher, Malcolm's ringtone filled the air. She grabbed her cell and answered with a cheery "Good morning" on her way to the living room.

"You must have been close to your phone." She could hear the smile in his voice.

"Right." She sat down on the sofa.

"We didn't talk about what we would do tonight."

She could hear him tapping something on the top of his desk. A pencil or pen. "What do you have in mind?"

"Well, there's this event at church tonight. It's a night for people to bless the single-parent families for Christmas. We don't have to go, if you don't want to." He almost sounded hesitant.

"Do you want to participate?" She'd love to bless single-parent families. In prior years, she bought gift cards for this ministry.

"I usually volunteer to work with the children while the parents go shopping with their gift cards. We also have a sort-of store for the youngsters to pick out presents for each of their family members. It's a regular Christmastime tradition for me." He stopped talking, and she knew he waited for her answer.

"I've never done anything like that, but it sounds like fun." Alanza heard him release a breath he must've been holding.

"Great. We'll be playing with the kids, too, so wear jeans and comfortable shoes. I'll pick you up about six p.m., if that's all right."

"I'll be ready."

That was something to look forward to. She loved kids. And doing something like this with Malcolm would reveal how he was with children. Something she really needed to know before giving him *the* answer.

She worked all morning helping the other chef, Marco, a second cousin. His main sous-chef called in sick. Some kind of winter malady was going around. She prayed none of her family or Malcolm's would catch it. Although she enjoyed working in the kitchen, she was happy when one of the other cooks showed up to fill in before the lunch crowd arrived. This allowed her to go back to her regular position at the register and getting ready for customers. Today, she needed to roll more silverware bundles.

Ever since Malcolm's first visit to the restaurant, she'd gotten into the habit of looking toward the door whenever someone came in between one and two, his usual time of arrival. Knowing they were going to be together tonight and he was picking her up early, she didn't figure he'd come in for lunch, but she automatically glanced up whenever she heard the front door open.

When her gaze traveled there the third time, Malcolm walked in. She couldn't stop the smile that spread across her face. She was busy going around the dining room, giving iced tea refills to diners.

Her mother approached and took the pitcher from her. "Go see Malcolm. I'll finish this. You can take your lunch break and eat with him, too. Tell him it's on the house."

Surprised, all she could do for a moment was gape at her mother. Then she leaned toward her and whispered, "Thank you, Mamma."

Right after she reached his usual table, they both sat down. Ignazio arrived right away.

"Dr Pepper?"

"Of course." Malcolm glanced at Alanza. "Do you want something to drink?"

"Yes, I'll have iced tea with some orange slices. Thank you, Ignazio."

Ignazio nodded and left.

"I didn't know if I'd see you at lunch today." She sounded eager, but she didn't care. He was quickly becoming an important part of her life.

Malcolm reached across the table and placed his hand, palm up, close to her. She slipped her hand into his, and he gave her fingers a gentle squeeze. "I really didn't plan on coming for lunch, but the closer it got to noon, the more I wanted to see you. You look so beautiful today."

Alanza laughed. "In my work clothes?" She appreciated hearing him say that—again!—all the same. "Mamma sent me over here and told me to take my lunch break with you."

His eyes widened, and he glanced over at Jacolin, who was pouring iced tea and talking to a couple. "Wow. I didn't expect that. So she's had a change of heart about us?"

"I believe she has." Alanza smiled at him. "She even said lunch is on the house."

When Ignazio returned with their drinks and to take their order, Malcolm asked her if she wanted to share a pizza.

"Sure."

"What kind would you like? Pepperoni, Italian sausage, chicken Alfredo..."

"No, none of those." She remembered the one he'd had Uncle Stefano prepare just last week. "I'd like one with spinach, artichoke hearts, mushrooms, basil, and extra mozzarella."

His eyes twinkled with his smile. "That's what I ordered when I went off-menu last week."

"I know. I've wanted to try it since then. You seemed to enjoy it so much. If it's as good as it sounds, maybe I can talk Poppa into making it a regular menu item."

A smile spread across his face. "That would be wonderful."

"Maybe we can name it after you." She laughed.

"That won't be necessary." He looked up at Ignazio. "A large pizza with spinach, artichoke hearts, mushrooms, basil, and extra mozzarella please. And two salads."

When the pizza came, Malcolm slid two slices on to Alanza's plate. "You can eat two, can't you?"

"Of course. I grew up on pizza." She took her fork and cut off a piece, blew on it for a moment, then ate it. "Hmmm. It's delicious."

"I'm glad you like it, but I eat my pizza this way." He picked up a large slice, folded it, and bit off the end.

"I don't do that until it cools down a little. I don't know how you can eat and drink hot stuff without burning your tongue."

He smiled and winked at her. "I'm talented that way. After a few more bites, he put his pizza down. "So we eat pizza differently. I can live with that."

For a moment, that comment stopped Alanza. Then she nodded. "I can live with it, too."

After the words left her mouth, she realized they sounded almost like a commitment. *Maybe it was.*

MALCOLM HAD IGNAZIO box up the rest of the pizza. He'd take it to the break room at work, where people were always bringing food in to share or looking for something to eat. Maybe Cantalamessa's would get a few new customers.

He really didn't have a lot of time for lunch today, but he'd wanted to see Alanza. For much of the evening, their attention would be diverted by their responsibilities. Sharing the pizza had been a good thing. It felt like a step forward in their relationship. He certainly hoped so.

At times during their lunch, they just enjoyed their food while gazing at each other without a word. Each time, he saw deeper into her heart. His love for her was growing at a supersonic pace, while the time he had left before he had to leave for Australia shrank at the same rate.

Lord, keep guiding my steps in Your timing.

The rest of the afternoon sped by. He had to work fast to get everything done. When he returned from lunch, he brought his duffel bag into the office and stuffed it under his desk. Before he left, he locked his door and closed the blinds. After quickly changing into a T-shirt, jeans, and running shoes, he pulled on his suit jacket and hurried to the car. If he left now, he could miss most of the rush hour traffic.

He barely pulled his car into the parking place in front of Alanza's apartment by 6 p.m. He didn't even have to ring the doorbell. She opened the door before he reached it. He loved

what he saw. He'd seen her dressed for work and dressed for an evening out, but Alanza in jeans and a long-sleeved T-shirt was altogether different. She looked more relaxed. And more beautiful. This was the way she would look relaxing at home when... if... they got married. *Lord, I thank You for bringing her into my life. Your will be done.*

She turned back toward the foyer closet to get her long coat.

ALANZA LOOKED AT the large number of cars in the parking lot when they arrived at the Grapevine campus of Way of Life Church. Most were older models. A few looked like clunkers. She whispered a prayer that they all would keep running for a long time.

When she and Malcolm went into the back of the sanctuary, she noticed that most of the people were single moms but there were a few single fathers, too. The singles' pastor was explaining plans for the evening. Each family would receive an envelope with gift cards in it, according to how many members were in the family. When the parents all left, volunteers would accompany the children into the education building and gather in the fellowship hall.

Malcolm leaned close to whisper. "You and I can go ahead to the fellowship hall and help get it ready."

They slipped back out and Malcolm took one of her hands. They walked across the open space between the main building and the education building. Alanza was glad she'd put on her warmest long coat. The sun had set and a stiff breeze tried to push the cold through their clothes. She shivered.

Malcolm pulled her closer, his arm around her shoulders. That helped a lot. He was like a furnace.

There were festive decorations on the walls of the fellowship hall and a large Christmas tree in one corner. Alanza smiled when she saw the tree's decorations, which had evidently been made by children. A pile of games and sports equipment waited in the middle of the floor. Tonight could really be fun.

A woman walked toward them. "Malcolm, who is your friend?"

"Another volunteer." He turned his attention toward Alanza. "This is Mary Mulligan. She chairs the Night of Blessings. And this is my girlfriend, Alanza Cantalamessa."

Mary's face lit up even more, and the usual conversation about Alanza's family restaurant ensued.

Alanza glanced around the room. "You're doing a great job."

"Not alone. I have a good committee and lots of volunteers like this one." She indicated Malcolm.

"What do you need us to do? This room looks like it's ready for the kids."

Mary smiled. "It is. I'm going to use the two of you right now in the stores."

She led the way down a hallway to a large room. "This is the store for the older children and the younger ones will shop next door. They are the largest classrooms we have."

Alanza was amazed at the wide variety of items, still in packing crates. Labels on some of the boxes indicated they held

electronics and sports equipment. She couldn't tell what was inside the other containers. Two lines of long tables stood close together in the middle of the room.

Malcolm noticed her looking around. "Those tables are the store and storekeepers will be between the tables. The kids can go down the other side of both lines."

"Can the two of you set up the store?" Mary looked straight at Malcolm.

He nodded. "Sure can."

"I have other people setting up the store for the younger children." She motioned for Malcolm to join her near the door.

What's that all about? Alanza moved to one of the unmarked boxes on the side of the room not far from the door. As she opened it, she casually eavesdropped on their conversation. She probably shouldn't, but she wanted to know what was going on.

"I've had to put out an emergency call for more volunteers. The truck with the shipment you ordered from Mattel just arrived, and we'll need all the help we can get so it's unloaded and set up in the other room." Mary laid a hand on Malcolm's arm.

"I'm sorry." He sounded a little upset. "I insisted that it be delivered this morning. I'll find out what happened. And I can call for backup if you'd like."

"Do you know anyone who can come right away?"

"I'll try." He took out his phone and made two calls. When he was finished, he turned to Mary. "My sister and father should be here in about ten minutes. I stressed how important it is?"

Malcolm returned to Alanza. "I have to go check on a delivery. Do you mind continuing to open the packages and putting the boxes with similar things close together?"

"Yes, I can do that."

"I should be back in a few minutes."

After Malcolm and Mary hurried away, Alanza moved some sports equipment to one spot as she mulled over what she'd overheard. Malcolm or his family must have donated a lot for the stores for the children to "shop" for gifts. At least they donated whatever was in the late truck. This was an example of what he told her last night about his family blessing others.

Generous went on the positive side of her list. Caring went right below it. Malcolm seemed to have as many layers as a large onion and she'd only seen a few of them.

When Malcolm returned, he moved with the precision and speed that can only come from experience in doing the task at hand. The stores were ready when other volunteers brought the children into the fellowship hall. Alanza and Malcolm waited for them, along with two other people who worked in the younger children's store. Most of the volunteers who brought the kids into the hall led other activities for them.

One woman stood by the door with a clipboard. She called out names and assigned each child to one of the store volunteers.

Each child had a list of family members and their ages. Alanza's was an 11-year-old girl. She took her around the store as she picked out gifts for the three people on her list. When they finished, they took the gifts into the wrapping room. The gifts would be wrapped, with tags attached and put into a white bag with the girl's name on it. All the bags would be stored alphabetically in another room, ready for the family to pick up when the parent arrived.

Alanza was impressed. The whole evening was well-organized. The gift cards she had purchased for this ministry in the past was one thing. Meeting the children and helping them select gifts for their families brought her feelings of Christian

love to a whole new level. As she talked to the children, she realized how blessed she was and how great their needs were. A few times, she had to fight back tears after helping a child.

After a couple of hours, Mary had Alanza and Malcolm trade places with the two volunteers who were working with the younger children. That was so much fun. Helping the little ones choose gifts was a totally different experience. Sometimes, they had no idea what to get, so she had to offer some ideas. She received many hugs and several kisses on the cheek.

As often as possible, she glanced over at Malcolm with his charges. His interaction was so mild-mannered and kind. *He will make a wonderful father. The kind I want for my children.*

13

$\mathcal{A}$re you tired?" Malcolm asked Alanza as they left the church parking lot.

"Exhausted." She laughed. "But it's a good kind of exhausted. I know why you always volunteer for this. It was great. Meaningful. Fun. I've always bought the gift cards and felt I was doing something special for people in need. But meeting these children has given me a whole new perspective. I'll definitely be volunteering for this next year."

Her excitement warmed his heart. Sharing a local mission project with Alanza and seeing it touch her heart made him love her more. His heart could hardly contain the emotions and spiritual growth this aroused.

As they pulled into the parking lot of her apartment, she turned toward him, her eyes glowing. "I'm exhausted, but I'm

also so keyed up I won't be able to go to sleep for a while. Do you want to come in?"

"Sure. Do you feel like making hot chocolate? Or maybe I can help you."

She knew he was using the cocoa as an excuse to stay longer. "What is this? Do you have an addiction to hot chocolate?" She laughed to be sure he knew she was just kidding. "Let's go in. There's time."

The wind was brisk as they got out of the car. He did his best to shield her from the worst of it as they mounted the steps to her front door.

"Give me your key then put your hands back in your pockets to keep them warm."

They hurried through the door and quickly shut it to stop the cold air from chasing them in. After taking off their coats and hanging them up, they headed to the kitchen.

He rubbed his stomach. "I don't care if the cocoa isn't fancy. I just want something warm in my belly."

She laughed at that. "Okay, hot chocolate milk and marshmallows it is then."

This time she warmed each oversized mug of milk in the microwave. She left enough room at the top to add a lot of miniature marshmallows.

"Let's go sit in the living room where it's more comfortable." She headed that way.

He followed and made sure to sit as close to her as he could. She relaxed, and he draped his arm across her shoulders.

"Ahh, this feels good." She sipped her cocoa and took a big bite of the melted marshmallows.

He followed suit. "And this tastes just right."

They set their mugs on the coffee table.

"What was your favorite thing tonight?" He knew what his was.

"I loved helping the children choose gifts, especially the younger ones. But probably the best part was that we did it together."

He smiled. "That's my favorite part, too, sharing all of it with you."

"Whenever I spend time with you, I learn more and more about you that I like." Her smile mirrored his.

His face turned thoughtful. "Alanza, I want to apologize for what I did when I gave you the hair bow. I shouldn't have attached such an important question to it. It was a gift." He hoped she understood he was retracting the question.

"Yes, that question has been on mind ever since you asked me." She leaned forward and took another drink of hot chocolate. "I'm actually trying to keep a positive and negative list, so I would know the answer."

That hit him right in the solar plexus, like the kick from a horse. He hadn't meant to make her life harder. *What a mistake to make!* When he took a drink from his mug, it didn't soothe him as it had before. What would it take to undo the damage he might have done to their relationship?

He got up and started to pace. "I've been trying to court you the way a woman should be wooed. I guess I've made a mess of that."

She stood. "I didn't say that. I really like you, and spending time with you, getting to know you, has been wonderful. Fun."

He let out a breath. "I'm glad I haven't completely ruined everything." He stopped in front of her. "What do you want in a husband? Would that be a better question?"

"I can answer that one." She resumed her seat on the sofa, folding her legs up beside her. "I want a man who is godly, who has an authentic relationship with Jesus."

Check.

"I want a man who is kind. Who has a gentle side. Who is intelligent, caring, and honest." She recited each attribute as if she were reading it off a piece of paper. "You seem to be all of these things."

Check. Except maybe not completely honest. Lord, help me to tell her in a way that doesn't scare her away!

He sat back down on the sofa but a little distance away from her this time. "I've been courting you at a fast pace for a reason. A reason you don't know."

"What reason?" She didn't look too happy.

"I felt I needed to keep some information to myself until you got to know me better. I didn't want to scare you off at the beginning." *Oh, Lord, that didn't come out right...*

Her eyes widened. "So you've been keeping a secret from me."

"Uh, no. Well, maybe. Sort of. I just haven't brought it up."

"How do you 'sort of' keep a secret? You either have one or you don't." Her green eyes flashed with outrage.

"Just hear me out, please." He leaned forward with his forearms on his thighs and stared at his hands, clasped between his knees. "Okay, so when I became the Vice President of Global Resources, I received an assignment outside the U.S."

"Where outside the U.S.?" Her voice seemed calmer now but he still did not dare to look at her.

At least she seems interested. So far, so good. "Australia."

"I've always wanted to visit Australia."

He could hear the smile creep into her voice, so he looked over at her.

"I saw you the first time about three weeks before this promotion. I already wanted to get to know you. But I also had pledged to God that I wouldn't date casually. I wanted Him to bring to me the woman He wanted me to marry. I wondered if you might be that woman. Because I was so drawn to you."

"I was drawn to you the first time I saw you, too, Malcolm." Her voice was soft.

He could tell she wondered where this conversation was going. "I spent most of the night with God, the night before I asked your father if I could ask you out. Asking Him. Communing. Listening. I received assurance that it was all right to pursue a relationship with you." *God told me we were made for each other. But are you ready to hear that?*

"Okay. What else?" *She must understand there's more to the story.*

"I was the main person who worked out the deal for our company to open an Australian office. The board of directors wants me to go there for six months to make sure everything is established the way we want it to be."

"When will you be leaving?" She reached over and covered his clasped hands with one of hers.

"I'll have to be there by the end of January."

"So you wanted to court me and establish a relationship before you left." Her phone rang just then. "Excuse me." She went into the kitchen to answer it.

He hoped it wasn't important. It was past ten.

She dropped back down on to the sofa and sighed. "Another of the sous-chefs just called Mamma to tell her she's sick. So I need to go in early tomorrow to fill in for her."

"I'm sorry to hear that. Do you want me to leave now?"

She shook her head. "No. I want to hear the rest of whatever you've been keeping from me."

Malcolm took a deep breath. *Here goes.* "I'd like for you to go to Australia with me as my wife," he blurted out.

"Your wife?" She stared at him incredulously. "So that's what this is all about. Seeing me every day. All the gifts. You're trying to win my heart, so I'll marry you before the end of January. Right?"

"Right." He covered his face with both hands and dropped his head.

An elongated silence hung between them. All he could do was pray that she would accept his explanation at face value.

Finally, she turned toward him, and reached out to touch his cheek. He raised his head to gaze at her.

"I just have one question."

"What's that?" Hope surged within him.

"What else are you not telling me?"

"Nothing. That's it. It's all out in the open now."

She stood. "You've given me a lot to think about."

He also rose to his feet. "There's just one more thing."

Heading into the foyer, he took a wrapped package from his coat pocket and came back to her. "I have a gift for you."

"I'm not sure whether I should accept it or not. I haven't decided if I can go along with all of this."

"It's just a gift. Part of my wooing you. I wish I had more time—believe me, I do. But since I don't, I wanted to give you this gift today."

She sat down and he put the package in her lap. She picked it up and turned it over and over. She shook it and listened. But

it made no sound. Finally, she started to carefully remove the bow, tape, and paper. A black velvet box, about six inches square, dropped into her lap. She pulled the top open and lifted out a sterling silver, heart-shaped jewelry box with a large, scripted letter "A" engraved on top. She stared at it before opening it. The inside was lined with purple velvet.

"This is really pretty, Malcolm. Since my initial is engraved on the top, I guess I'll just have to accept it and say thank you... Wait. Isn't Bella's name Arabella? You could give it to her." She closed the lid, put it back inside the gift box, and handed it to him. Stood. "Since it is so late, and I have to get up early, we need to say goodnight."

He set the box on the coffee table and pulled her into his arms, hesitating to give her time to tell him to let her go. But she didn't. So he just held her close in a warm embrace until she finally stepped back.

"I thoroughly enjoyed tonight, even with the secrets you told me."

"It was a very special night for me, too." He dropped a quick kiss on her forehead and headed out the door.

He left with a hopeful heart. At least, she hadn't rejected him outright.

14

Thursday – Six Days Before Christmas

lanza awoke with a sense of anticipation. *Today is the day.* After spending time in prayer about the situation, she could no longer deny her love for Malcolm. He was handsome, smart, kind, courteous, generous—wonderful in every way. She was blessed that he wanted her for his wife. He hadn't said the words *I love you* yet, but she was sure he would soon. Especially since they needed to marry before he moved to Australia.

Australia!

It was too soon to tell her parents. She and Malcolm had details to iron out before they did that. Even if they waited until after Christmas to tell their parents, they could put together a wedding in less than a month. Alanza wasn't one of those women who had dreamed about her wedding since she was a young girl.

The world moved fast. There was no reason why wedding plans couldn't. Even now, she wasn't dreaming about the actual wedding, but what would happen afterward...

One step at a time. Today, she would wear his tartan in her hair. She didn't know any reason for Malcolm not to eat at the restaurant today. How should she fix her hair to display the bow to its full advantage?

Alanza sang as she showered and blew her hair dry. She'd have to wear the regular employee uniform because she'd be filling in for a sous-chef. At least, she wouldn't have to wear a *toque blanche.* The tartan clip would hold her hair back. She wished she could wear regular clothes today instead of the uniform.

Unable to cover her head against the cold, she parked as close to the door as she could. Mamma was already there. When Alanza walked into the kitchen, she looked up and immediately noticed the bow.

She stared at it. "Where did you get that plaid bow?"

"Do you like it?"

Mamma smiled. "It's very pretty."

"Malcolm's sister made it for me."

It wasn't exactly a lie. She'd just left out some information. *The way Malcolm had.* Then it hit her. She didn't elaborate because she didn't want her mother to question what was going on in their relationship. Malcolm had withheld information until the time was right. Now, she understood. *I owe Malcolm an apology.*

She put on a voluminous apron, washed her hands, and went to the station Marco pointed out. Chopping vegetables was mindless work. The repetition monotonous. While she worked, she let her thoughts wander to Malcolm... and the secrets he revealed last night.

"Watch out!" Marco screamed as he walked toward her. "You almost chopped off the tip of your finger. If you can't keep your mind on your work, I'll have to get someone else to do it."

"I'm sorry, Marco. I'll be more careful." She pushed thoughts of Malcolm to the back of her mind and focused on the vegetables.

Marco stood beside her a moment, evidently watching to make sure she was doing it right. Finally, he went back to his cooking.

When she finished all she needed to do for him, she relaxed. Almost time to open the front door. She washed her hands and went into the break room to hang up her apron and check herself in the mirror. After anchoring the clip more firmly over the hair she'd rolled and pulled up atop her head, she freshened her makeup.

Alanza marched out to unlock the door, then returned to work the register. Now she could daydream about Malcolm for a while. She felt cheeks reddening. Hopefully, Mamma would think it was from the heat of the kitchen.

SOMEONE AT WORK must be cold. The heat was turned up past Malcolm's comfort level. He had to close the vents in his office and take off his suit jacket. Eventually, he had to close his office door, too. The company leased two floors in one of the most

prestigious older office buildings in Fort Worth. Unfortunately, each floor had a single thermostat. Malcolm wished he could control it.

He glanced at the clock. *One p.m.* Since he was at a good stopping place in his work, he saved the file, both to the office cloud and his laptop. He grabbed his jacket from the coat rack and settled it on his shoulders, straightening it so he'd look okay when he went through the office to the elevator.

He'd been able to focus on the project, but when he got into his car, his thoughts immediately returned to his favorite subject. *Alanza.* After their serious discussion last night, he felt they had reconnected before he left her. At least, he hoped so. She'd told him she'd enjoyed their night together and she didn't pull away when he kissed her forehead. That had to be a good sign.

When he opened the door to Cantalamessa's, his eyes were drawn to the woman he loved. A smile spread across her face when she saw him, too. A good sign.

She's wearing the tartan clip! Thank you, Lord! His smile widened. He wanted to run to her, throw his arms around her, and kiss her right there in front of God and everybody. He'd been holding back so long. Then he laughed internally. He was such an idiot. A month wasn't *so long.* It only felt that way. A demonstration of public affection wasn't what he wanted for their first kiss.

He headed toward "his" table. The waiter almost beat him to it, carrying a Dr Pepper and the menu.

"Thank you, Ignazio. No wonder you're such a popular guy around here."

"Do you need to look at the menu today?"

"No, thanks. I'd like the eggplant parmesan. I haven't had that yet."

"A salad, too?" Ignazio held his pen poised over his pad.

"Yes, thanks, with the house dressing this time. A little bird told me it's very good." His eyes twinkled and Ignazio smiled.

"A six-foot tall bird, I presume?" He chuckled and left for the kitchen.

Malcolm looked straight at Alanza. He loved the way the bow looked. It felt like she was announcing to the world that she belonged to him. Like she was off limits to any other man because she was wearing his tartan. Bella told him Alanza understood what wearing a Scot's tartan meant. He could hardly wait until this evening. When he got back to the office, he'd call her to see where she wanted to go. Or maybe she'd want to stay in since they were so tired last night, and she had to start work early this morning.

She didn't look tired. Instead, she was glowing.

"Hey there, Mal, may I sit with y'all?" A vaguely familiar female voice broke into his thoughts.

He glanced up and almost grimaced. *What in the world is she doing here?*

A former coworker named Jessica sat in the chair closest to him, even though there were other chairs at the table. She had changed a lot since they had worked together some time ago. She still had Texas-big hair dyed blonde, but now, she was wearing too much makeup, too tight clothes, and long, pointed fingernails painted fire engine red. Her slender fingers looked like talons.

Malcolm casually scooted his chair as far away from her as he could. "It looks like you already are, even though I didn't say you could."

She ignored his blunt hint and moved her chair closer to his. Then she put a hand on his arm. "'Member how close we were when we worked together?"

What kind of question was that? He remembered a lot about her. How she threw herself at him over and over. How each time, she acted like she didn't hear his rebuff. Just as she was doing right now. They'd never, ever been close. *What's wrong with this woman?*

"What I remember, Jessica, was you trying to get me to date you. It didn't happen then and it won't happen now. Got it?" Would she ignore his gruff brush-off this time, too? *What's it going to take to get rid of her?* Malcolm was afraid to look over at Alanza. *What must she be thinking?* "I also remember hearing that you got your clutches into an older wealthy man and got married. Does that sound familiar?"

She swatted him on the shoulder and leaned even closer. "That's old news, darlin'. We're not together anymore. I want to reconnect with you and continue our relationship. Word is you just got a promotion and a pay raise. That makes your sweet self even more desirable." She gazed up at him and batted her huge, overdone false eyelashes. "Not that you aren't desirable all on your lonesome."

She had a way with words that didn't make a lick of sense. Malcolm glanced at Alanza. Her expression revealed just what she thought about what she was seeing. *Great! Just great! This idiot woman has sent my relationship with Alanza about five steps backward!* He needed to get rid of Jessica pronto!

She reached up and turned his face toward her.

The nerve! Malcolm jerked away as if Jessica had slapped him.

She completely ignored his reaction. "I'm sittin' here, darlin', not over there." She started to pout, then noticed the direction he'd been looking. "Wait. Do you have something going on with that poor working girl? Don't worry. I'll make sure she leaves you alone so you and I can be an item again."

"We were *never* an item, except in your crazy brain," he hissed.

Ignazio came over to the table. He had probably overheard Malcolm's last words. He didn't bat an eye. "Here's your salad, Mr. MacGregor." He glanced at Jessica. "Does your companion want something to eat?"

"She's not my companion."

She leaned closer and batted her eyes up at Ignazio. "He's just bein' silly. You just walked in on a little lovers' spat. I'll have whatever he's havin'."

Ignazio looked as if he didn't know what to do.

"Go ahead and bring her the same thing and put it on my bill. But take this back and have my food packaged to go."

When Ignazio left, Malcolm turned toward her. In an angry whisper, he spat out his words. "I. Do. Not. Want. To. See. You. Ever. Again." He extricated himself from her clutches. "I'll be back."

"Oh." She sat up and clasped her hands in her lap. "Okay, darlin'. I'll wait for you."

"I'd rather you just left." He glanced toward the register—and Alanza was no longer there.

He hurried to the men's room and dawdled for several minutes. He peeked out to see if the way was clear, but Jessica still sat in the chair. Drinking *his* Dr Pepper.

Lord, why is this happening right now? I don't want to cause a major scene in Alanza's family's restaurant. I can't think of anything else to do besides taking lunch back to the office.

When he went back to the table, he sat on the other side, out of her reach. Looking closely at her, he detected signs of desperation in her eyes. "What happened between you and your husband?"

Jessica started to cry. Her mascara ran down her cheeks with her tears. "He divorced me. He decided I only married him for his money. But he's so wrong about that. I loved him."

"If you love him, why are you here?"

Her mouth puckered into a pout. "I thought you were my friend, Mal."

He hated it when she called him by his nickname. He never let anyone outside his family call him that. "Remember when I suggested you try going to church?"

She frowned. "Yes, but I'm not into that religion stuff."

"You might learn something that could help you with your problems."

She shrugged, and her low neckline revealed more of her cleavage than he wanted to see. He turned his eyes away from her.

"I don't have problems that being with you wouldn't cure."

Well, that didn't work. She was off her rocker if she thought he'd ever want to be with her in a romantic way. *Or any way at all!*

"Look, Jessica. I'll pay for your lunch, but when my food comes, I'm leaving, and I don't want you following me."

She gave a forced smile. "I know where you work. Your assistant told me where to find you."

Just wait until he got back to the office. He'd have Jessica banned from there.

Ignazio came back with Malcolm's food packaged for take-out and Jessica's food on plates.

"Thank you." Malcolm looked at Jessica. "Are you going to eat it here?"

She smiled at Ignazio. "I want mine carry-out, too."

Malcolm grabbed the bill from the tray, picked up his take-out bag, and headed toward the register. Alanza was back, and she looked as if she'd been crying. He wanted to wring Jessica's neck.

He laid the bill on the counter and reached for his billfold to get his credit card.

He didn't realize Jessica had followed him until she said, "Hi, there. I'm Jez. You know, like Jezebel." She held out her hand as if she wanted Alanza to shake it.

When Alanza didn't, Jessica said, "Thanks again, Mal, for asking me out to lunch."

She leaned closer to him and planted her very red lips on his cheek before she walked away. He could feel the greasy lipstick. He pulled out his white handkerchief and wiped his cheek. Sure enough, it was smeared with red. "I did *not* ask you to lunch," he muttered.

Alanza quickly turned around and hurried away again. Her mother rang up the purchase and gave him the receipt to sign. She wasn't smiling.

He didn't blame her. He was sure Jessica had destroyed all of the headway he'd made with Alanza's mother. Maybe even Alanza, too. Thanks to that crazy Jessica, Malcolm knew he was in deep water. And he didn't know how to get out. Somehow, he had to find a way.

15

$\mathscr{A}$s soon as Malcolm arrived at work, he called Christine into his office. "I brought my meal back. I'll be eating it here."

"Okay." She smiled at him. "I'll keep people away until you're finished. Unless it's Mr. Talbot."

"Sounds good." She started walking to the door.

Malcolm called out to her. "Wait please. I need you to make a note to yourself and let the receptionist know that Jessica Loring, or Jez as she calls herself now, is not to be admitted into the office. If you need to call security to get her to leave, do it."

Christine looked confused. "She told me she was an old and dear friend of your family."

"You can't believe anything she says. Sometimes... she's delusional."

"I'll let the front desk know right away."

Malcolm tried to work while eating his lunch. He really did. But his mind kept returning to all of the drama at Cantalamessa's. *Jessica's crazy. She needs to be in a psych ward.* He heaved a deep sigh. *Not really.* He'd caught a glimpse of something in her eyes... desperation, maybe. *Or something like that.* That's why he mentioned church to her. He had the feeling she'd been hurt by someone at church or some other Christian. He probably should pray for her instead of putting her down. She made him angry, but that didn't give him the right to blacken her name.

He called Christine on the intercom. "I'd like to speak to you for a moment please."

She quickly arrived with her pad and pen and sat in the chair in front of his desk.

"You won't need those." He laid his fork on his napkin. "I misspoke earlier. Jessica *does* have problems, but I shouldn't have said what I did about her. She needs help, not a putdown."

"Does this mean we should let her in if she comes back?"

"No, that still stands. It means I'm going to pray she gets the help she needs, that's all."

Christine stood. "Praying for someone is a help." She quickly exited.

After he finished eating, he tried to work, but Alanza's tearful face haunted him. What could he do to fix things? He picked up his phone and called her cell. Again. No answer. Was she still working? Surely not, since she started early this morning.

He called the restaurant. After three rings, a voice he didn't recognize answered. "I'd like to speak to Alanza, please."

"I'm sorry. She left over an hour ago." The man hung up.

She's probably home. Malcolm dialed her number again. Ten rings, no answer. Either she was napping... or she wasn't answering *his* calls. Since he wasn't accomplishing much at work, Malcolm decided to go home. He'd change into more comfortable clothes, then go to Alanza's. Surely she'd open the door if he rang the doorbell.

When he pulled into his parking space, Eric's car sat in the adjoining spot. His roommate had only taken three days to come home. Something else for Malcolm to deal with. *Lord, help me do this Your way.*

He opened the apartment door and smelled an enticing aroma emanating from the kitchen. He dropped his things off in his room before heading there. "So the prodigal has returned home."

Evidently, Eric hadn't heard him come in. He jerked around with the hot pot from the stove in one hand, a dripping spoon in the other. "What are you doing home so early?"

"I was just going to ask you the same question." Malcolm laughed bitterly. "I wasn't getting much done, so I left the office."

Eric set the pot back on the burner, put the spoon on the counter, and grabbed a few paper towels to clean the drips off the floor. "I thought it was time to come home and apologize to you."

"I figured you were staying away because of that." Malcolm went to the fridge and popped open a Dr Pepper. "Want a soda?"

Eric threw the dirty paper towels into the trash can. "Sure. Are there any Cokes left?"

"Should be. You're the only one who drinks them." He chugged down some Dr Pepper.

Eric turned the burner off and put a lid on his pot. "Well, anything's possible. You could have had someone over who drank Coke."

"Nah." Malcom smiled at his roommate. "I spent a lot of time at her place."

"Surely not overnight." Eric knew Malcolm's strong Christian convictions.

Malcolm frowned. "Of course not."

"I didn't think so." Eric glanced down at the floor. When he raised his head, his face was deadly serious. "One reason I came home was to apologize to you."

That caught Malcolm by surprise. "What for?" He thought he knew, but he might be wrong.

"For contacting your family and siccing them on you." Eric rubbed his hands together, then crossed his arms. "I felt they should know what was going on since you weren't listening to me."

Malcolm pulled a chair out from the table and dropped into it. "I was completely blind-sided, yes... And I was very angry."

"Yeah, your dad told me." Eric took off his apron, the one Malcolm got him for Christmas a couple of years ago. It read, "I'm a MANLY cook." They had a lot of fun that year.

"When did you see him after he came over?"

Eric sat in the chair across from him. "Late yesterday. When he and Bella arrived to help unload the truck with the toys, another truck full of stuff had just pulled up and was in line to be unloaded. He knew they'd need strong guys to help, so he called me and a few of his golfing buddies. If he hadn't, things wouldn't have been ready for the kids when the event started."

Malcolm shook his head. "I had no idea you were there. Wish I'd known."

"Your dad and I didn't talk until we were finished." Eric took a napkin from the stack at the other end of the table and started fiddling with it, shredding it into a pile. "Look, things were moving so fast, I was afraid Alanza was only after your family's money. I know you don't flaunt it and a lot of people have no idea. I was just trying to save you."

Malcolm stared out the window. "I'm not angry anymore. But you really were out of line. And you shouldn't have done it. I've never, ever, done anything like that to you. And never would in a million years."

"I know. That's why I wanted to say I'm sorry. I can't take back what I did, but I really am very sorry... even repentant."

"Repentant? What do you mean?" He wasn't sure where Eric was going with this conversation.

"Just what I said." His roommate stood up and glanced down at him. "I know I've slowly drifted away from the way I was raised. I remember my *coming-to-Jesus* experience, but I'd walked away from it. Sunday, I'm going back to church. I want my life to be the way it's supposed to be."

Malcolm jumped up. "Hallelujah! I've been praying for that for a long time." He clapped Eric on the shoulder.

"You want to do something together tonight?"

"Man, I wish I could, but something happened today, and I need to go check on Alanza."

"Okay." Eric smiled. "Your dad told me how much he likes her. He said she was good for you. I'm glad for you."

ALANZA HAD CRIED herself out. She washed her face with cold water, trying to get the red to disappear. She could hardly believe what happened today. That woman, that Jez, was a bigger secret Malcolm had kept from her. When she asked if he was keeping other secrets, he told her he wasn't. This was like a stiletto to her heart—and not a high heel. She reached for the tartan bow clip to throw it in the trash when her doorbell rang.

She didn't want to see anyone right now. And she didn't want anyone to see her. She looked through the peephole in her door and all she could see was red roses. Surely Malcolm wouldn't come to her with flowers and another set of lies. That wouldn't work. She'd give him a piece of her mind.

Grabbing the doorknob, she opened the deadbolt with her other hand and slung the door open. She could barely see the grill of his car behind him because of the profusion of flowers. There had to be at least three dozen red roses in a large, cut-glass vase.

"I don't want to see you." She started to close the door on him.

He stuck his shoe in the doorway to stop it from moving. "I need to talk to you, Alanza."

"I'm not interested in anything you have to say, Mr. I-Don't-Have-Any-More-Secrets."

"Please, Alanza. Let me in for a few minutes anyway."

Hearing the pleading note in his voice, she backed up and let him in.

When he entered, he looked haggard and he wasn't smiling. "I'm really sorry for what happened."

"You sure kept *that woman* a secret from me. Are there any other secrets I should know about?" *I will not cry in front of him... I will not cry in front of him... I will not...*

"We need to add water to this vase." Malcolm's voice was husky as he set the vase on the coffee table, as if it suddenly became very heavy.

"Let's wait until I decide whether to throw them at you... or not. Or maybe just throw them in the trash!"

He looked shocked. And hurt. "Would you let me tell you about Jessica before you decide?"

Alanza frowned. "Jessica? Who's Jessica?"

"The woman at the restaurant." He grimaced. "The one I *did NOT* invite to lunch."

Alanza sat in one of the wingback chairs across from the sofa to keep him from sitting beside her. "You know, Malcolm, I wouldn't have even let you *into* my apartment if it hadn't been for Ignazio. He told me he was there when she sat down with you. He overheard you saying you didn't ask her to lunch. So tell me about this Jez... Jessica." She frowned, crossed her arms, and waited.

"She worked at the first company I did after I graduated from A&M. Back then, she wasn't like she is now. She did flirt and try to get me to go out with her, but I wasn't interested even then." He sat with his forearms on his thighs and clasped his hands between his knees. "I kept pushing her away, and eventually, she was fired. I heard she hooked an older, wealthy man, and they got married."

"Did she know how rich your family is?" Maybe she was beginning to understand.

"I've never mentioned that to anyone, but somehow, she found out. Maybe she looked it up on the Internet. She's very computer savvy." He began to relax.

Alanza nodded. "That explains a lot."

"I never saw her after she married… until today. I hardly recognized her. She didn't dress like that when we were coworkers. From what she said today, evidently, the old guy she married divorced her." He leaned even farther forward, wanting Alanza to feel his sincerity, his honesty. "Alanza, you have to know that you are the only woman for me. All I could think of at the restaurant was how to stop her from fawning all over me and you seeing that. I knew you'd think what you did. Then later, when I saw that you'd been crying, it broke my heart. I wanted to go behind the counter and comfort you, reassure you."

She gave a quick, harsh laugh. "That would have really upped the drama, wouldn't it?"

"When I paid, I could see what your mother thought about me." He heaved out a ragged breath. "I don't know if I'll ever get back in her good graces."

"She's a helicopter mom. She hovers over me like I'm still a little girl."

"Do you understand now?" He gazed into her eyes.

"Yes. All the time, even though I was hurt, I knew it was so unlike you. Is that why you made your lunch to-go?"

He nodded. "I didn't want to cause a bigger scene at your parents' place. I've done a lot of thinking instead of working this afternoon."

She leaned forward, listening intently. "What were you thinking about?"

"Us and the possible effect it would have on our relationship... but also something more."

"What else?"

"I noticed something about Jessica. All that act was bravado. I caught glimpses of fear and vulnerability in her eyes. I had asked her to go to church when we worked together. I asked her today if she went to church and she said she wasn't into all that 'religion stuff'. I feel bad for her, even after how she behaved today. I really want to start praying for her. God can reach her or send one of His followers to help her find Him. Would you please pray with me... about her? Jessica, I mean... not Jez. She's somewhere inside that hurting woman."

She moved to sit beside him on the sofa. He took her hand in his. As they prayed, he knew he wanted to pray, too, for Alanza, for their future children, and for others, for the rest of their lives.

After the prayer, he stood and pulled her up beside him. "I've been wanting to do this since I first saw you. I was waiting

until you wore my tartan in your hair. Because you know what that means."

He gazed into those beautiful green eyes and watched them darken into pools of emotion. He slowly lowered his head, and her eyes closed. He gave a gentle kiss on each eyelid, then each cheek, and finally sought her lips. A soft sigh met his. He took his time and kissed her thoroughly until both of them were breathless. Before, he'd felt like the tartan bow was his brand on her, but it wasn't. This kiss—a fusion of their emotions and spiritual beliefs—was the real brand. No one else could see it, but he was sure she felt it, too.

When they finally parted, her face glowed with the brightest smile he'd ever seen, and tears glistened in her eyes. He wiped them away with his fingertips.

"Why are you crying?" he whispered.

"They're tears of joy." Her soft words went straight to his heart. "I never imagined anything like that kiss."

"Neither did I," he said huskily. And went in for a repeat.

After that kiss, she glanced over at all of the roses. His gift for today. "Let's take these to the kitchen and rescue them before they start to wilt. I plan to enjoy them as long as I can."

16

Friday – Five Days Before Christmas

Time was flying by and now, Malcolm feared Mrs. Cantalamessa might take away her approval. Alanza planned to talk to her today, to explain about Jessica. All Malcolm could do was pray that she would understand.

Lord, I trust You. I've felt your guidance through all that has happened. I don't want to marry without Alanza's parents' blessing. And time is really short. I know I'm not supposed to worry, but, Lord, it's hard not to. Help me leave it all in Your hands. In Jesus's name, amen.

He turned back to his laptop with a lighter heart and a more settled mind. He had to finish several things today. Concentrating on the project at hand, he lost himself in the intricacies of the spreadsheets. He thrived on planning the

details needed for a specific project. It was a special gift from God.

When Christine arrived, she knocked on his door with his favorite coffee, as she did every workday morning. He needed it right now. He'd come in very early to make up some of the time he lost yesterday.

"Come in." He looked up from his computer as she opened the door.

"I brought you your coffee and one of those apple fritters you like from the doughnut shop. Since you left work early yesterday, I knew you'd be here early." She placed paper towels on his desk and set the large Styrofoam cup and the pastry on them.

"Thank you, Christine. You're so good to me." He smiled and reached for the coffee.

"Just what time did you come in this morning?" She crossed her arms like a teacher about to scold a student.

He laughed. "I'd rather not say." He took a bite of the fritter.

She remained standing beside his desk, crossing her arms and tapping her toe.

"Six. Or so."

"Then it's time for a break." She turned toward the door. "Enjoy." The word drifted back to him just before she exited.

Maybe he should take a real break. He got up and stretched the kinks out of his back. Getting so involved in a project, he often forgot to move at all. *Not a good idea.* Gazing out his window, he saw a brilliant winter day with deceptively bright sunlight that wouldn't remove the chill at all. Tree limbs were not moving, so at least there wasn't a wind right now. Maybe it would stay that way. If he and Alanza went out this evening, he didn't want them to fight a cold wind.

On the TV news last night, the weatherman had a forecast of an unusual white Christmas this year. He wouldn't believe it until he saw it. Most of the snow in this part of Texas came in January and February.

Faither's ringtone brought his attention away from the window. "Hello?"

"Malcolm, your brother and sister and their families will arrive today. Your grandmother wants to have a dinner here tonight with all the family. And your Alanza."

Why not? "Sounds good to me. Let me run it by her."

"Bella says they're all eager to meet the woman who finally captured your heart."

Malcolm heard the teasing humor in his father's voice.

"I hope they won't try to grill her about every little thing in her life. Maybe you could caution them."

"I'll try. I don't know what good it'll do, but I'll try."

"Thanks, *Faither*."

After disconnecting the call, he rang Alanza. She usually didn't go to work until around ten, so she should still be at home. *Hope she's not in the shower or something.* Why did he open his mind to that picture? He pushed it away. Time enough for that after the wedding.

The phone rang several times, and he'd decided to hang up when she finally answered. "Good morning, Malcolm. Did you sleep well?"

"Yes, but I had to get up early to come in and make up for leaving early yesterday. What about you?"

"I fell right to sleep. And I had the most delicious dreams." There was a new, flirtatious tone in her voice.

He knew she wasn't talking about food. "I'm glad because *Faither* just invited us to a family dinner tonight. Not a party, just a regular family get-together. My married brother and my married sister and their families will arrive for their holiday visits. Bella says they're all eager to meet you."

For a moment, she said nothing. Then, he heard her take a slow, deep breath. "Wow. I didn't expect to meet your whole family so soon."

"They don't bite. They'll love you, just like I do."

"O...kay. Do we need to dress up for the dinner?"

"Just nice casual... like last time." He hoped she would feel more comfortable this time. She would need to get used to his family home sometime. Might as well be tonight.

"What time will you pick me up?"

"Six-thirty. We won't eat until seven-thirty. That'll give you time to meet all of them, get to know them a little."

After they hung up, he tried to get back into his project. *We need to get married soon. I need to be able to concentrate on finishing things up here before leaving for Australia. So few weeks left until then.*

MALCOLM LOVED SEEING the tartan clip in Alanza's hair. She wore dark brown slacks and a beautiful red turtleneck that

matched the red in the ribbon. As they drove toward the Trophy Club, he asked her how things went with her mother.

"I was worrying so much about meeting the rest of your family, I forgot to tell you before." She beamed at him.

The smile on her face made him consider pulling off into a parking lot so he could take her in his arms and kiss her again. But smudging her makeup before they arrived at the house might not be the best idea. They'd have plenty of time for that when he took her home.

"Mamma and I were in the break room talking. I explained what you told me about Jessica. Right in the middle, Ignazio came to clock in. He heard the last few words before we stopped talking. He assured Mamma that what you said about what happened was true."

"Good man, Ignazio." He liked her cousin now more than ever.

"After I told her the rest of it and how we prayed for Jessica, she told me how much she respected you. She even said she'd be praying for her, too."

"That's good. Jessica really needs all the prayers she can get." He went through the gates and turned on to the long driveway to the house.

"I'm sure Mamma will tell Poppa all about it, so he'll be praying, too."

He pulled up near the side door. In the shadows, he leaned close to Alanza.

"I want to kiss you again... but I don't want to mess up your lipstick before we go in."

She must have heard his longing because she leaned closer and kissed his waiting lips. Or maybe she longed for the kiss as much as he did. With her lips firmly resting on his, she threaded

her fingers through his hair at the back of his head. *Oh, yes! So silky thick...*

The console between them made an embrace difficult, but with both arms around her, he drew her closer to him. The kiss took on a life of its own. He forgot they were sitting in the driveway. All he was aware of was the feel of her in his arms and the growing desire...

The sound of someone knocking on his window brought him out of his daze. Bella stood there, laughing, then turned back to the house. Leaving them alone.

He settled Alanza back into her bucket seat. "Sorry I smudged your makeup."

"Really?" She stared at him until they both laughed.

"No. Not really."

"It's all right. I can reapply the lipstick." She turned the sun visor down and opened the lighted mirror. She found a clean tissue and wiped her mouth.

He watched every move she made. She was beautiful without any makeup on, but he knew she wanted to wear some to meet his siblings and their families.

After carefully applying fresh lipstick, she turned back and forth, looking at the effect. "That will do."

He went around to open her door. When she got out, he placed his arm around her waist. Leaning close to her ear, he whispered, "You do know there are signs of a passionate kiss that lipstick doesn't cover, don't you?"

The blush he liked so much rushed up her cheeks all the way to her hairline.

"I think you're cute that way." He opened the door, and they entered the house.

Bella waited just inside the door. She hugged him and whispered close to his ear. "Way to go, big bro'."

Now he felt heat fill *his* cheeks. He hated that part of being a redhead. Now the whole family would see his blush. Maybe he could blame it on the cold air outside, especially, if anyone started razzing him about it.

Bella hugged Alanza then hurried ahead of them toward the den. "They're here."

Excited voices greeted them when they walked into the room.

"Unca Mal!" His three-year-old nephew rushed toward him with his arms held high. "Up!"

He caught the tyke in his arms and swung him around.

Laughing, Alanza moved out of the way.

Malcolm stopped with the child in his arms as he faced her. "This is my nephew, Angus."

Angus patted Malcolm's cheeks as he led her toward one sofa. The man and woman sitting there stood to meet her.

"This is my sister and her husband, Isobel and Alastair Stewart. Isobel is two years younger than me. This little rug rat is theirs." He glanced around the room. "Where's Kirsty?"

His sister was still gazing at Alanza. "She's taking a nap. Daddy has worn her out playing with her. And Mal, where are your manners? Who is this beautiful woman?"

He laughed. "Sorry, but I thought Bella told you *everything*. This is Alanza Cantalamessa, my girlfriend."

Isobel hugged her. "I hear you're more than just a girlfriend."

Alanza bestowed a bright smile on her. "I certainly hope so."

Everyone else in the room rose to their feet as Malcolm and Alanza approached them.

Angus gave one of Malcolm's ears a hard yank. "Ow!" He pulled the boy's hand away and Alastair rushed toward them.

"That's his new thing right now." He reached for his son. "Come to Daddy."

At first, Angus seemed to be defiant, clinging to Malcolm. Holding his nephew against his chest opened a longing in his heart. He had always known that he wanted to get married and have children someday, but now that the wedding was on the horizon, his paternal feelings erupted like a geyser. He could have a son of his own soon. Maybe within a year. He and Alanza might have a baby by then. The enormity of the reality hooked him and held on. *Whoa!*

Finally, Angus turned to his father and held out his arms.

Malcolm glanced around to find Alanza. She was talking to his younger brother and his wife.

ALANZA WATCHED MALCOLM approach. "Bella introduced me to Craig and Heather."

"Yes, big brother." Craig grinned at him. "We waited long enough to meet this woman. I can see why she was able to catch you when so many others couldn't."

Alanza could hardly believe her ears. "I didn't chase—"

Malcolm put his arm around her. "You have that backwards, lil' bro'. I chased her. Can you blame me?"

Alanza wanted to sink right through the floor.

Malcolm's father came to the rescue. "Let's all sit down and relax. We can get acquainted while cook finishes getting the meal on. Won't be long now."

Of course, as they talked, a number of questions came up.

"So, where did you two meet, Alanza?" Isobel's question didn't surprise her. In fact, she worked out an explanation before he picked her up that evening.

"My family owns an Italian restaurant on Highway 10 in Euless. Cantalamessa's Gourmet Pizzas and More. One of Malcolm's friends at work told him about it, and he started coming pretty regularly for lunch."

All eyes turned toward Malcolm. "How long ago was that?"

He smiled. "About a month ago."

"But…" Isobel didn't look. "From what Bella told us, I assumed it was quite a while longer. Aren't you considering marriage very soon?"

Malcolm stood up. He had a commanding presence. Alanza was so proud of him as he faced them.

"I'm going to tell you about it, but please, you can't talk about it to anyone outside this room. We haven't shared the details with Alanza's family yet. We haven't had a chance. We intend to tell them in a couple of days."

He explained all about his promotion, having to move to Australia for six months, and how he'd sought God about the woman He'd prepared for him.

Alanza was pleased to see his family wasn't fazed by that part. *Thank you, Lord! You prepared a husband for me and gave him a family that walks with You and understands having a relationship with You here on earth.*

Isobel smiled. "I didn't know you were engaged. May I see your ring?"

Alanza didn't know what to say. "Well, we're not actually—"

"We're not engaged." Malcolm smiled at Alanza. "I haven't proposed yet. We need both of our families to understand God's hand in our lives. We don't want to get married without their blessings. I feel we have your support, but we need the same understanding from the Cantalamessas."

Alanza looked down at her bare ring finger. Now she felt strange. Knowing God was in this and trying to trust Him in all things. Knowing she wasn't engaged, even though they'd talked about the timing for their wedding... *Lord, help me believe and trust You for the timing.*

AFTER A WONDERFUL meal, Malcolm's grandmother excused herself from the family gathering in the den again. As Mrs. Campbell climbed up the stairs in the foyer, Alanza watched her through the open doorway. She looked a little tired. Maybe all of the boisterous talking and laughing was wearing on her. Alanza whispered a prayer for her.

After about half an hour, she returned, carrying a small box in one hand.

"Malcolm, you don't know about this, but when your mother was ill, she gave me something. She wanted it for your bride. I've kept it safe all these years."

She held everyone's attention.

"She gave me things for all four of you children. Isobel and Heather have things that she gave me for them. This is for Alanza. To welcome her into the family. To show her how much we all accept her. To reveal how much your mother prayed for her for years."

Mrs. Campbell stopped in front of Alanza and slowly handed the box to her. It wasn't wrapped like a present, but it looked like a jewelry box.

Tears pooled in Alanza's eyes. "Thank you." She kissed Malcolm's Nanna on the cheek.

Malcolm moved closer to her and watched as she lifted the lid. A beautiful, intricately carved cameo lay nestled in the velvet-lined box, accompanied by a gold chain and a tartan ribbon.

Alanza lifted the piece of jewelry out. The cameo was hanging from the ribbon.

Mrs. Campbell moved a little closer to her. "The original ribbon was falling apart, so when I found out Malcolm was in love with you, I replaced it with the tartan one. It matches the bow clip in your hair. And if you want to wear it on a chain sometimes, I put one of mine in there for you, too."

Alanza was overwhelmed. The love she felt from Malcolm's family filled her with gratitude—and love for them in return. Now if only he could receive the same kind of acceptance from her family on Sunday.

17

Saturday – Four Days Before Christmas

alcolm arrived at Alanza's house at 8:30 a.m. On the way home from dinner at his family's house last night, she told him she heard that the Way of Life's Arlington campus was doing an outreach program today. After the way they both enjoyed volunteering for the single-parent families' event, she wanted to participate in this one. He did, too. He put on his oldest clothes, but he knew they were still far better than those worn by the people to whom they would be ministering. That was one reason he drove his family's old Jeep.

When Alanza opened her door to him, his heart gave a leap. This gorgeous woman loved him. Just as he loved her. *Could life get any better?*

She glanced behind him. "Where's your car?" Then she shivered.

"Let me in, so we can get out of the cold, and I'll tell you."

She stepped back then quickly closed the door behind him.

Before anything else, he gathered her close and gave her a heartfelt kiss.

"Umm, that's nice." Her eyes had a dreamy expression. "I could do that all day."

"So could I." He dropped another quick kiss on her waiting lips. "But if we do, we won't ever make it to the laundromat."

He looked at her clothes. "I think both of us are overdressed. I tried to dress down, but these are the oldest I have." He held up one foot. "I did find some really old running shoes to wear."

She laughed. "I think I would have thrown that pair away, but they're just right for going to the laundromat today."

"There's a Goodwill store on the way there. We could stop and get some older clothes to wear so we don't stand out so much. And you need to bundle up really well. I drove *Faither's* old Jeep, instead of the Beemer. It probably needs new door and window seals. Some of the cold air seeps in. I don't want you to freeze." He gave her another big hug.

"I have some shoes I wore when I painted the apartment." She looked down at her feet. "I'll go change into them then I'll be ready to go."

While he waited, Malcolm looked at the walls around him. He hadn't really noticed the colors before. Most apartments had walls painted some shade of white or light tan. Alanza's were different colors—smoky blue in the living room, mustard yellow with some decorative stenciling near the ceiling in the kitchen, and soft, pistachio green in the spare bedroom. It all made her apartment more personal and homey.

Alanza walked back into the living room, wearing sneakers splattered with different colors of paint.

"Did you do all the painting in the apartment?"

She nodded. "It took me a while to convince the manager to let me. I promised I'd make sure the walls were returned to that blah light tan they were when I moved in, and I promised I wasn't going to move out anytime soon."

"How long ago was that?" He could just imagine him having to help her paint before they moved to Australia.

"Three and a half years. Right after I graduated from college." Alanza went to the closet and pulled out a heavy sweater, a scarf, and her long coat.

"Maybe we can find coats at Goodwill as well as jeans and sweaters."

WHEN THEY DROVE east on Airport Freeway, Alanza pulled her scarf up over her nose and clutched her coat tighter around her. "You weren't kidding when you said cold got into the Jeep."

"Sorry about that. It won't be so bad when I turn off the freeway. I'll be driving slower." He reached down and turned the heater up as high as it would go.

"It's invigorating, for sure." She watched cars, trucks, and businesses whiz by. "I'm not sure what to expect when we get to the laundromat. Do you know anything about this outreach?"

He moved to the right lane to take the next exit. "I haven't been on one of these missions, but I have a buddy who has. I called him last night."

After turning right down the street, he quickly reached the Goodwill store. Although it was only 9 a.m., the parking lot held several older model cars. Although the Jeep looked like a clunker, his father kept the engine in tip-top shape.

After he parked, he turned toward Alanza. "My friend said the church provides coffee, bottles of water, doughnuts, fruit, packages of snack crackers, laundry detergent, and quarters to run the machines. The volunteers really don't go in preaching. They just serve the people—helping them with their laundry and trying to get to know them. They do offer to pray for anyone who wants them to. Things like that."

"Sounds interesting."

They entered the store and headed toward the clothing department. Right away, Alanza found old worn Wranglers to wear instead of the designer jeans she had on. Even though they were her oldest jeans, she didn't want any women she met at the laundromat to feel poorer because of her. When they both reached the checkout line, they had enough clothes to keep them warm while they were helping with laundry.

The laundromat was close to several rundown apartment buildings. Leaving their regular clothes in bags under the back seat, Malcolm locked the Jeep.

The other volunteers had already arrived. The outreach pastor for the Arlington campus assigned a task to each volunteer. "Remember, try to connect with the people you help on a personal level."

She and Malcolm were there to help with loading the washing machines and then moving the clothes to the dryers.

"Help yourself to a doughnut and coffee, if you want." The pastor picked up a cup and took a sip.

While they ate and drank, they got acquainted with the other volunteers. Some were older, some were teen-agers, but most were in their twenties and thirties.

Alanza sat on the edge of the folding table to eat her doughnut. She gazed out the window at a nearby apartment building. Evidently, they didn't have laundries inside like many apartment complexes did. Hers actually had a laundry room in each apartment. What a blessing she'd never thanked God for.

A very old woman, bent with age, was dragging a large duffel bag through the dirt toward the laundry. *How in the world will she get everything home when the clothes are dry and folded?* Everything on the bottom will get dirty.

Out of the corner of her eye, she noticed someone moving toward the door. She turned her head and saw Malcolm hurry outside and jog up to meet the bent-over woman. He stopped to talk to her. He must have charmed her because her face lit up into a smile, awakening her inner beauty. He lifted the large duffel and slung it over his shoulder then offered his bent arm for her to hold as they walked to the laundromat.

He kept up a running conversation with the woman while he helped her fill three washers with her clothes. She looked amazed when he produced three little boxes of laundry detergent and enough quarters for all three machines.

"Bless you, young man." Her voice trembled. "You're such a blessing to me today. Since you're doing this, I'll be able to buy my medicine this week."

Tears streamed down her face. Malcolm talked to her as they sat side-by-side in the hard plastic chairs by the wall across from the washers.

Leaning against one of the washing machines on the other side of the room, Alanza caught an occasional word. "Alone... baseball... arthritis."

A car pulled up in front and parked beside the Jeep. A young woman opened her trunk and lifted out a plastic laundry basket.

Alanza went out to meet her. "Here, let me help you."

The woman jerked back, fear filling her eyes.

"It's okay," Alanza reassured the woman. "My church is doing an outreach program here today, to share blessings with people. I'd like to help you with your laundry." She glanced at the large box of cheap laundry detergent in the trunk. "You can leave your box of detergent here because we have laundry soap and money to run the machines. And snacks, too."

The woman looked at Alanza as if she were crazy. After staring at her a few moments, she let Alanza take the basket. Two more were wedged into the trunk.

As she headed into the laundry, the woman opened a rear passenger door and brought out three little children. They all went into the laundromat and Alanza kept up a running conversation while she loaded a washer with the contents of the basket and started it. That allowed the woman to watch her children. One she carried on her hip. The other two clung to her jeans-clad legs.

She showed the woman where the food was and the volunteer there warmly welcomed the young family.

Alanza headed back out to the car to retrieve the other two baskets. Stacking them, she carried both at once, her arms straining under the weight. While she sorted the clothes and loaded three more washers, she watched the mother and her children eat some doughnuts. Perhaps they didn't have enough food at home. They seemed hungry. Alanza's heart ached.

The volunteer in charge of the snacks insisted that she have something to eat, so Alanza took an apple and a bottle of water.

All around the laundromat, other volunteers were helping young families and older people. Quite a few came in looking like they carried the weight of the world on their shoulders. As they were helped and had something to eat, many began to stand up straighter. Some laughter rang through the room.

Lord Jesus, help me remember this day. And please show me other ways I can help people. In Jesus's name, amen.

As the day wore on, many people were ministered to—whether by just doing their laundry, freeing up money for other needs, or praying for those who asked for prayer. Alanza often watched what Malcolm was doing. He seemed to be seeking out people with the greatest needs. More than once, he accompanied someone to the apartments across the street to carry their clean clothes for them. Her love for him grew. He was genuinely good and tender, with a heart for others. He walked out the faith he espoused.

Once, she saw him walk out with a young woman who was rail-thin. Malnourished perhaps. She had seen Malcolm encourage her to take some snacks before she left. When they reached the Jeep, they went around to the driver's side. Alanza watched as the woman threw her arms around Malcolm and hugged him. She didn't know what was happening, but when Malcolm headed back inside carrying their Goodwill bags, the Jeep backed up and drove away. She was sure she saw the thin woman driving.

Before he got busy with another group, she went to him and pulled him aside. "That woman who drove away in the Jeep. What was that all about?"

He looked a little sheepish. "I'm sure the pastor wouldn't agree with what I did, so I did it privately." He pulled her close and whispered in her ear. "She lost her job, so she lost her car. She's been trying to get another job, but she doesn't have a way to get there if it's not nearby. This isn't a neighborhood with many jobs that pay enough to live on, even if you're single. I'll be meeting her sometime after Christmas with *Faither* to transfer the Jeep title to her. I called and asked him first, of course. We may even meet her with a good used car to trade her for the Jeep instead."

She hugged him. "So how will we get home, hero?"

He shrugged. "I'll call a cab."

By mid-afternoon, they started cleaning up.

Malcolm watched Alanza through the smudged window as she walked an elderly woman to her apartment, carrying her basket of clothes. When she came back across the street, she stopped and looked intently toward the west, then turned back to reach for the door of the laundromat.

A man's tattooed arm snaked around Alanza's waist. His other hand held a knife to her throat. Then they both disappeared from Malcolm's sight.

Malcolm shouted, "Where's security?!" The church provided a plain-clothes security guard for events like this.

"Just went into the bathroom," someone answered.

Without stopping to listen to the chatter that ensued, Malcolm sprinted out the door. As he rushed around the building, he saw Alanza and her assailant about to cross the vacant lot behind the laundry. He didn't have the knife at her throat anymore, but he still held it in his hand. She tried to fight him off and he was yelling at her. "Be still, ya dumb broad. Don't wanna hurt ya, but I will if I hafta."

Without missing a beat, Malcolm ran full-out toward the two. *Please faint! You need to get out of the way! Please just fall down!* He prayed for God to impress on Alanza the need to somehow free herself from the man so Malcolm could tackle him. As he ran, he saw the man weaving, still struggling with Alanza, yelling slurred nonsense. Maybe he was high.

The security guard ran toward them, too, yelling. "Let her go! Let her go!"

When Malcolm was only a couple of strides away, Alanza crumpled to the ground.

Instinctively, the man let her go so she wouldn't pull him down with her. Malcolm took that opportunity to take a flying tackle. It brought the man down, cursing and fighting. They tussled in the dirt. He tried to slash at Malcolm with the knife. There was a wild look in his eyes. Before the security guard got near them, his blade skipped and jumped across Malcolm's left shoulder, penetrating several times. In the adrenaline of the moment, he didn't feel the wounds until blood began to soak his shirt. The guard ran faster and reached the attacker. In a moment, he tased the man, disarmed him, and had him in handcuffs.

Sirens approached. *Finally!*

Alanza dropped down beside Malcolm, pulled off her scarf, and pressed it against the knife wounds. "You saved me! My hero!"

The adrenaline rush was gone and pain sliced through his shoulder. He looked up at Alanza. "Did he hurt you?"

"I may have some bruises tomorrow but nothing permanent."

"Thank You, Jesus."

"I agree." She smiled down at him.

"I prayed He would give you the idea to fake a faint. That's all I could think of to distract that guy when I got close to him."

She laughed. "I wondered where that thought came from, but it seemed like a good idea. If you hadn't been close, I was going to kick him where it hurt so I could get away. My brothers always told me to do that if I ever got into a bad situation. I figured this was a seriously bad situation."

He tried to laugh, but the movement caused his knife wounds to hurt even more. "I sure hope those brothers like me when we meet tomorrow."

"They have no other choice now."

Two patrol cars and an ambulance came over the curb and bounced across the field to where they waited. The security guard turned the attacker over to the police and the EMTs headed toward Malcolm and Alanza.

While the paramedics checked his vital signs, a police officer came over. "We'll need to get statements from both of you."

One paramedic turned to the officer. "We need to take him to the ER. He's lost a lot of blood."

"Okay, miss, I guess we'll talk to you now and question your friend later."

"No!" Alanza was emphatic. "I'm going in the ambulance with my fiancé."

Malcolm wanted to laugh. But his shoulder was throbbing. They weren't engaged yet, but that was probably the only way the paramedics would let her go with him. *Smart thinking.*

BECAUSE MALCOLM'S KNIFE wounds were deep, they took him right in. The police questioned Alanza in one of the empty hospital rooms and she told them what happened. Now, she prayed in the waiting room. The police were still waiting so they could talk to Malcolm.

A nurse came to the waiting room and asked for the people who were with Malcolm MacGregor to come on back. The policemen escorted her as she followed the woman. She felt glares and stares from other people in the waiting room. *I wonder if they think I'm a criminal.* She shrugged off the uncomfortable prickles on the back of her neck. She didn't care. She just wanted to make sure Malcolm was all right.

The nurse led her into a private room, but asked the police to wait outside. The doctor told her that Malcolm was lucky—no arteries or nerves were hit in the attack, but Malcolm had needed about twenty stitches.

"We'd like to give him a couple pints of blood to replace what he lost and keep him here overnight for observation."

Alanza nodded, but Malcolm interrupted. "I'd like to go to home."

"You should be monitored throughout the night."

"I insist." Malcolm's words were strong but not combative. "My brother-in-law is a doctor and my sister is a nurse. They're in town for the holidays. They can take care of me."

The doctor glanced at Alanza.

She smiled, relieved. "I'll make sure he's well taken care of."

As soon as the doctor left, the officers came in. "Miss Cantalamessa, would you give us some privacy?"

She glanced at Malcolm.

He nodded. "When they're finished, we can call my father and someone will come to get us."

As she wandered the nearby halls, she came to a gift shop. Framed in a window was a display of teddy bears with bandages on various parts of their bodies. One even had a cast on its leg and a tiny crutch attached to one paw.

A bear with fur was the same rich auburn color as Malcolm's hair sat in the middle of the display. It wore a bandage on the same shoulder as Malcolm's knife wounds. The word "Hero" gleamed in bright embroidery on its chest. It held a large, puffy red heart with both paws. *How perfect!* She immediately went in and bought it. The cashier even put it in a nice gift bag for her.

After her purchase, she headed back toward Malcolm's room, arriving just as the officers were leaving.

When Alastair arrived to pick them up, she told him she'd like to be dropped off at her apartment.

"No." Malcolm was adamant. "I want you at the house with me tonight."

Alastair shrugged.

Alanza protested. "I won't have anything to wear or any of my things. My hairbrush. My toothbrush."

Malcolm pulled her down to sit beside him on the edge of the hospital bed. "I'm sure there will be plenty of things for you to wear and use. Please stay with me. I *need* you."

How could she say no to that plea? She couldn't.

In the car, she and Malcolm both sat in the back. Alastair didn't seem to mind.

"I got something for *you* this time." She handed him the gift bag.

"Should I tell you, 'But it's not Christmas yet?'"

"No."

He tried to open the bag and winced. "Help me please. The anesthetic is wearing off. My shoulder *hurts*."

She took the bag back, lifted out the bear out, and placed it on his lap. "I saw this and had to get it. To remind you that you're a hero. You saved my life."

When he smiled at her this time, the twinkle was back in his eyes even though he was in a lot of pain. "Does this mean you're courting me now?"

She laughed. "What do you think?"

He pulled her toward him with his good arm. The kiss he planted on her this time was way beyond what the others had been. Breathless didn't come anywhere near what she felt. He still hadn't said the three little words yet. But that didn't matter today.

"I love you higher than the Texas sky, Malcolm."

"And I love you even more," he whispered, "dear Alanza."

18

Sunday – Three Days Before Christmas

The guest suite was as opulent as the rest of the MacGregor home. Alanza had been afraid she'd have nightmares about what happened yesterday, but she hadn't. *Thank You, Jesus.* Maybe she had been too exhausted to dream.

Last night, after they had a good meal, her parents called her. They'd seen something about the incident on the 10 o'clock news. She hadn't even noticed a TV news crew at the scene. Everything had been surreal. Poppa wanted to know if she really was all right—because he and Mamma had watched her climb into the back of an ambulance. They tried to insist on coming over to the MacGregor house to pick her up right then. But Maxwell heard her side of the conversation and asked if he could speak to her father. He was able to calm Poppa down, then he invited her parents over for brunch after church today.

196 Lena Nelson Dooley

He understood Alanza wouldn't want to leave Malcolm, who felt too woozy from pain medication to go to church. The two of them would watch the church service on TV.

She had gone to bed really late. She and Alastair kept watch over Malcolm until his brother-in-law insisted she needed to go to bed. Malcolm was asleep when she last saw him. She'd kissed him goodnight and whispered, "I love you."

Even though she was not going to be physically in church, Alanza still wanted to wear something nice. Everyone else would be wearing their Sunday best when they returned. She and Bella were almost the same size, so Malcolm's sister put some of her clothes, along with some toiletries, in the guest suite last night. Bella wasn't quite as tall, so her russet-brown, wool midi-length dress fit below Alanza's knees. It brought out the green of her eyes. Bella even offered Alanza her own tartan hair clip. She knew Malcolm would be pleased to see it in her hair.

When she got downstairs, she was surprised to find Malcolm out of bed and dressed, wearing casual pants, a T-shirt, and soft V-neck sweater.

"Are you ready for breakfast?" He kissed her cheek.

All she wanted to do was pull him closer and weave her fingers through his thick, wavy auburn hair. But she didn't want to hurt his left shoulder. She could never hurt him in a hundred years.

"How did you get that sweater on without hurting your shoulder?"

He chuckled. "Slowly and carefully. Alastair is a good doctor. He said it should heal quickly. I might not even have scars. But I won't mind if I do. Saving you from that maniac was worth every cut and bruise." He grinned sheepishly. "I should

have remembered, though, that tackling someone without protective gear would leave me a little banged up."

He put his right arm around her and they went into the dining room, where brunch items lined the long serving table along one wall. The cold foods were in basins of ice and the hot foods were under heat lamps. An absolute cornucopia of enticing flavors.

"Are we the only ones eating right now?" She hadn't heard the sound of anyone else in the house. Of course, it was so large, she wouldn't hear a thing if they were in one of the wings.

"Except for Alastair and us, everyone else went to church. He's asleep, since he stayed up most of the night with me. Usually, the kitchen staff gets Sundays off, but they wanted to stay and make sure we had plenty to eat when we got up. And for your parents when they come over."

She smiled. That kind of devotion could not be bought. She was sure the staff must be treated like family. "How long have they worked for you?"

"As long as I can remember, for the most part. We seldom have anyone leave and when they do, it's usually because they want to get an education or something like that."

They went into the den with their plates and drinks and sat at the game table to eat. The large-screen HD TV almost made Alanza feel as though she was at the service. When there were close-ups, the worship team and pastor were larger than life. The sermon "Trusting God" really spoke to her heart. The pastor used Psalm 37:4–5 for his text, one of her favorite passages. She could see God's hand on her and Malcolm during the last nine days. Guiding both of them individually. It seemed longer than that because they had spent so much time together.

Getting to know each other, ministering together, and falling in love.

When the service was over and their plates empty, she turned to Malcolm. "God does work in mysterious ways, doesn't He?"

He pulled her closer to him and stole a kiss, which she gave gladly. "With us, He has."

They took their dishes to the huge kitchen. The kitchen maid and cook scolded Malcolm for doing that. They both insisted they would've cleaned up after the two of them.

"I know. You're very good to us. But this didn't hurt me a bit." He gave each of the older women a quick hug. Smiles spread across both faces, and one of them blushed.

They heard several cars pull up to the side door that was closest to the warm kitchen.

"Y'all get outta here." Cook flapped her apron toward Malcolm to shoo him. "We need to get more food on the table."

The rest of Malcolm's family, along with the Cantalamessas, hurried out of the cold and down the hallway to the den. Several conversations accompanied them. When Alanza's parents caught sight of her, they rushed to embrace her.

Mamma looked her over, up and down. "I don't see any bruises."

Poppa gave Malcolm the *eagle-eye*. "I hope not."

Alanza laughed. "I'm sure I'll have a few little bruises, but probably not where you can see them." She moved closer to Malcolm, slipping her hand inside his right elbow. "Malcolm was a hero, saving me from getting hurt worse."

That made him blush. She loved it when he did that. Someday, she might tell him that. But not today.

MEALTIME WAS MERRY, with everyone getting acquainted. Malcolm watched as Alanza's parents gradually became more relaxed and cheerful. *Thank You, Lord!* He needed that. He wasn't sure how they'd take the information he and Alanza had to share with them today.

Faither told him that since they planned to reveal the rest of the information to her parents today, he would invite everyone else upstairs to the family home theater on the third floor to watch a Christmas movie. So Malcolm could be alone with the Cantalamessas.

After his family went upstairs, Malcolm invited Alanza's parents into the den. He'd considered the parlor, but it was too formal. He wanted all of them to be able to relax.

Alessandro sat in a recliner but kept it upright. "You seem to have something on your mind, Malcolm."

Before he could answer, Jacolin interrupted. "So does our daughter."

"Yes, sir." Malcolm leaned back on the sofa beside Alanza. "Sir, I'm sure you recall that I asked if I could date Alanza with marriage in mind."

"I do." He nodded. "And I said yes, if that was what she wanted."

Malcolm launched into an explanation about his almost all-nighter with God where He revealed Alanza was the woman He'd prepared to be Malcolm's wife. "After that, every time I

saw your daughter, I fell more in love with her. Like a heavenly gift from God."

Alessandro just raised his eyebrows a bit, but he didn't comment. So Malcolm continued to share all of the details just as he had rehearsed over and over in his mind—his promotion, the six-month assignment in Australia, the timing, the need to act.

He concluded, "I want to take Alanza with me."

Alessandro looked flustered.

"As my wife."

Alanza's father relaxed. "Let me get this straight. You want to marry my daughter in January, next month, and leave soon afterward to go to Australia and be there for six months."

The questioning statement hung in the air between them.

"Yes, sir."

Jacolin smiled at her husband. "Alessandro, when he looks at our Alanza, I see the same spark of love in his eyes as I've always seen in yours. He's never ogled her as many men have."

Alessandro lowered his head and put his folded hands between his knees. After a minute of silence, he raised his head and his eyes zeroed in on Malcolm's. "Would you promise me that you will love my daughter with your whole heart and protect her with your life?"

Alanza rose to her feet. "Poppa, he already loves me that way! And he's already put his own life in danger to protect me." Her eyes filled with tears. "He knew our time of courtship would be brief, so he has wooed me the way he feels every woman should be. He's even given me a gift almost every day."

A frown creased Alessandro's face. "Are you trying to buy my daughter's love?" he growled.

"I'd never do that."

Alessandro shook his head. "Let me pray about this until tomorrow."

"Yes of course. I believe the Lord will speak to you the same way He spoke to me."

When her parents left, Malcolm asked Alanza to wait in the den, telling her he needed to do something. When he returned, he had another present. This time, she didn't say anything about it not being Christmas yet.

She opened the gift, not worrying about being careful with the wrapping paper or bow. She lifted out a gold chain with an opal pendant surrounded by diamonds.

"Oh, Mal! It's beautiful!"

"It's an Australian opal." He grinned. "Symbolizing where we're headed."

"What if Poppa doesn't agree?" Her eyes filled with tears again.

"Remember the Scripture from this morning's sermon." He quoted it for her:

> *Delight yourself also in the* Lord, *and He shall give you the desires of your heart. Commit your way to the* Lord, *trust also in Him, and He shall bring it to pass.* (Psalm 37:4–5 NKJV)

19

Monday – Two Days Before Christmas

lanza stayed another night with Malcolm's family. This time she went to bed at a decent hour and slept all night. The emotional toll of the last couple of days had wiped her out, but being able to watch Malcolm's recovery encouraged her. Now, she clung to the Scripture the pastor and Malcolm had shared with her. *God, I truly do want to trust in You and allow You to bring it all to pass.*

As she walked down the staircase in the foyer, she watched the rain trail down the windows. It looked wet and cold outside. She was glad she and Malcolm would be staying in today.

The MacGregor family members all breakfasted together. She enjoyed watching Angus's antics. And ten-month-old Kirsty had really taken to her, cooing and gently grabbing her long black hair. They took her mind off her worries. *Poppa and*

Mamma HAVE to give their blessing. Have to. They have no reason not to. She also thought about the children she and Malcolm would have someday. She really hoped for a boy with auburn, wavy hair just like his. And a little girl with a sweet smile and disposition. She wondered how many children he might want. She wanted at least three or four. *So many things we still need to talk about!*

Her phone rang. She glanced at the screen. *Poppa.* She went into the foyer to have some privacy.

"My precious girl, I wanted to tell you first. Then I will talk to Malcolm." *What's that mean? Yes? No?* Her heart started to pound. "I prayed as I promised. And your mother and I are at peace about everything. The wedding, the time in Australia—all of it. I'm glad God brought such a man to marry you."

"Oh, Poppa! Thank you!"

"Now, Alanza, we have to hang up so I can call your future bridegroom."

She sat down on a step and cried tears of joy again.

Malcolm was walking through the halls, looking for Alanza, when his phone rang. "Hello?... Thank you, sir... Yes, of course. We can talk over the details when we're together again... I'm sure that will be fine... I need to talk to Alanza about this... Thank you, sir... Talk to you soon. Bye for now."

He pumped his right fist into the air. A wide smile spread across his face. *Thank You, Lord, for the blessing on our marriage from Alanza's parents!*

He found her sitting on the stairs in the foyer, sat down beside her, and wiped the tears from her cheeks with his fingertips. "Don't cry, darling. All is well. I told you we could trust God to bring about His plans for us. Remember what the Bible says." He quoted it for her:

"For I know the plans I have for you," declares the LORD,
*"plans to prosper you and not to harm you, plans to give you
hope and a future."* (Jeremiah 29:11 NIV)

Alanza giggled, feeling very silly for crying. Malcolm pulled
her close and kissed her.

Everything else faded away as their hearts entwined, their
heartbeats syncing. A spiritual connection she'd never imagined wrapped her in a blanket of completeness. Time and space
melted away and it was just the two of them in a special place
that she never wanted to leave. An eon later, but far too soon,
the wondrous kiss ended. She stared into Malcolm's blue eyes,
which were full of emotion. Bathed in the velvet force of his
amazing love, she could hardly breathe.

He stood, took her hand, and led her into the empty parlor.
They sat on the Queen Anne loveseat with his good arm around
her.

"Well, it's actually a good thing that we can't go where I
planned to take you today because we have a lot to talk about."

She smiled at him. "Where were you planning to take me
today?"

"Ice skating at Panther Island. Have you ever ice skated
before?"

"No. How can you ice skate in Texas except if you're playing
for the Dallas Stars?" She laughed.

Malcolm smiled. "They make an ice rink on Panther Island
at Christmastime. But it's good that we can't go. We have a lot
of plans to make."

She sighed. "I know. Where do we even start?"

"Well, I drew up a timeline we can use, if you agree." He
pulled out his phone and showed her a calendar. "We need to

be in Australia by January 29. That way, we'll have a couple of days to get settled before I have to start work. Maybe the first thing we need to do is pack up any personal belongings we want to take. Favorite household items. Anything that won't fit in our luggage. We can ship them ahead. Either air freight or on a ship."

"Won't that be expensive?"

He hugged her closer. "My company will pay for it. If there are a lot of things, they'll need to go by ship."

"Okay. What else?"

"If we get married on January 18th, we can have a ten-day honeymoon in Hawaii on our way to Australia. Does that sound good to you? Can we put together a wedding in twenty-three days?"

At first, she hesitated. *But look how far we've come in so little time! If anyone can pull it off, we can!* "You know, that sounds great, Mal. And I've always planned to wear my mother's wedding dress, so that part is taken care of."

"And I have a kilt tuxedo to wear. Actually, I have two different ones."

She threw back her head and laughed. "I didn't know they had kilt tuxedos." She tried to imagine the look.

"All the men in our family have them. Come upstairs and I'll show you."

"Isn't that bad luck?"

He laughed. "We don't believe in good or bad luck. We believe in God's blessings." He led her to his bedroom suite.

"I'm surprised you'd give up living here for an apartment."

"Alanza, I'm twenty-six. I don't mind staying here sometimes, but I like to be on my own."

"I understand. I'm two years younger than you but I value my independence, too."

He went into his closet and returned with two garment bags. He removed a tux from each one and laid them out on the bed. One had a plain white shirt, while the other had ruffles down the front above the vest. That one looked more like wedding attire to her.

She touched the tux with the ruffled shirt. "I'd love for you to wear this at our wedding."

"I will then. Now both of us have our wedding outfits all set." He raised an eyebrow and winked at her. "All the MacGregor men will be wearing kilts, you know."

Malcolm went to a bureau and opened the top drawer. "While we're up here, I have something for you." The box wasn't wrapped, so he opened the lid and lifted out a brooch. "This is a brooch to keep a tartan on your shoulder. All Scottish women have them."

He handed it to her. She studied the magnificent piece. It was larger than any brooch she'd seen before. Gold with an emerald in the middle and small pearls around the edge. "This is beautiful."

"Would you be willing to wear the tartan and brooch for our wedding?" He looked at her hopefully.

"If I had a tartan, I'd love to."

20

Tuesday – One Day Before Christmas

lanza gazed at the empty third finger on her left hand. *It's very strange to be planning a wedding and yet not be officially engaged.* Yesterday, she and Malcolm had discussed many details, but he still hadn't proposed. He had said he wanted to court her the way a woman should be wooed. *Shouldn't a proposal be included in that?*

She really wished he would make a formal proposal. She loved Malcolm enough to elope if that's what he wanted to do, but evidently, he wanted to have a wedding. And they both had the right attire for one.

She would talk to Mamma about wedding plans after Christmas. She didn't want to take away from the special celebrations of Jesus's birth. That should be the focus today and tomorrow.

After breakfast, Bella drove Alanza home. Malcolm rode along. Although he was recovering well, his shoulder wasn't up to driving quite yet. Alanza needed to get some of her own clothes, makeup, and other belongings. The whole MacGregor family insisted that she return to spend tonight with them again. In the evening, they would all attend the carols, communion, and candlelight service.

She really looked forward to that. She loved Christmas carols. She usually started playing them the day after Thanksgiving, but she had been so busy and spent so little time alone in her apartment this year that she hadn't. And she missed hearing them. A whole service dedicated to singing carols, followed by taking communion as a family, and ending with the candlelight service—that would be a welcome break from all that had been happening, especially Saturday's fiasco.

Her parents had agreed to attend the Grapevine campus service with the MacGregor family. Maxwell had invited them back to his house tomorrow for a mid-afternoon Christmas dinner. That way, they wouldn't have to plan a special meal just for themselves and Alanza. As they did every year, they closed restaurant Christmas Eve Day, Christmas Day, and the day after Christmas. Their regular customers were understanding. They had never shied away from sharing their faith. And, of course, Alessandro and Jacolin gave Cantalamessa's employees their regular pay, along with Christmas bonuses.

Alanza again stared down at her naked ring finger.

Her brothers served in the military and both were deployed overseas right now. They wouldn't be home until early January. But they could be here long enough to be in the wedding, if it took place on the 18th.

When she finished gathering her belongings, Bella drove them to Malcolm's doctor's office. Alastair wanted him to get a more thorough examination from his regular practitioner.

As they walked into the office, the receptionist and a nurse immediately came out into the waiting room and hugged Malcolm. Alanza knew he was caring and loveable, but she didn't expect him to get this kind of welcome.

"Here's our hero now." The receptionist spoke loud enough for the few other people in the waiting room to hear. All of them turned their attention toward Malcolm and Alanza.

They must have seen their "fifteen minutes of fame" on the news. Because she'd been so busy the last few days, she hadn't even checked social media. People might have seen it there, too.

The nurse went over to Alanza. "Are you all right? I heard the man was trying to kidnap you."

She hadn't heard that—and she didn't like being the center of this kind of attention. "I'm not sure what he wanted. He was not making any sense. Malcolm..." She lowered her voice, trying to keep everyone from hearing. "...is my hero. He risked his own life to get me away from that man. That's how he got... stabbed." She didn't know what else to call it.

"Come on back," the nurse told Malcolm. She picked up a folder from the counter. "Your fiancée can come, too."

Bella sat in one of the waiting room chairs and was leafing through a magazine. She looked up at Alanza and nodded for her to go ahead.

The doctor welcomed them into one of his exam rooms. He gestured for Alanza to take the chair and asked Malcolm to take off his shirt and sit on the exam table.

"So, you're engaged?"

They answered at the same time. "Yes." "No."

The doctor laughed and started taking off the bandage. "So, which is it? Yes or no?"

Malcolm gave a slight nod and looked at her as if to say *you answer.*

She cleared her throat. "Well, it's not official yet." Without thinking, she looked down at her empty ring finger.

Malcolm smiled. "But we're discussing a wedding."

"I see." The doctor patted Malcolm's wounds with a medicine-soaked cotton ball. "How bad does this hurt?"

Malcolm looked down at his shoulder. "Not too bad. Has it begun to heal?"

"You're young and you mend quicker than a man my age." He put a salve of some kind on gauze before taping it down across the cuts. "Come back in about a week, and we'll remove the stitches. Take a tub bath until then, so you won't get this wet."

Malcolm grimaced at that comment.

When they arrived at the MacGregor house, Alanza got out of the car first. "I should've thought to drive my car over here."

"Why?" Malcolm and Bella both asked at the same time.

She laughed. "So I can drive myself home."

Malcolm put his good arm around her shoulder. "Don't worry about that. Someone will drive you home. Maybe I will. The doctor didn't tell me not to drive."

"Men!" She knew how stubborn they could be. Her brothers taught her that. The doctor hadn't said he *could* drive either.

"When you finish putting your things in the guest room, come meet me in the parlor." Malcolm dropped a lingering kiss on her forehead. Even that sent delicious shivers down her spine.

She was back downstairs in less than ten minutes. Malcolm must want to talk to her about something important for them to be in the parlor alone.

"I'm here."

He arose from the loveseat they'd sat in before and gathered her against his chest. "If I have to wait until the eighteenth of January for the wedding, I'll have to take it easy on the passionate kisses," he whispered. His lips lowered toward hers, and she melted with his kiss. She knew what he meant.

When he finally pulled back, he smiled into her bright green eyes. "There are a few things I want to say."

Yes! Finally, a proposal! Her heart started to beat faster just thinking about it.

He sat on the loveseat, and she nestled close to his good, right side. "I hope you realize you won't have to work when we get to Australia. You aren't going on a work visa as I am."

"Okay." She wondered where he was going with this conversation.

"I want you to be able to follow all of your dreams. You love painting and creative writing. I want you to have time to do that. And I hope you want to be my wife and someday be a mother." He smiled down at her.

"Of course, I do."

His words awakened a place deep inside her. She'd spent much of her life doing what others needed or wanted her to, especially her parents, and she wasn't sorry about that. But there were hidden dreams no one except Malcolm knew about. She had art materials—oil paints, watercolors, brushes, a palette, colored pencils, a few blank canvases, sketch pads—many things like that. She knew she wanted to pack at least some of them to ship to Australia. She also had long dreamed of writing

a novel. Now, it actually seemed like that was possible. She hugged him. "That all sounds heavenly to me."

He rested his chin on the top of her head. "Our adventure in Australia could open a lot of new things in our lives. I'm really looking forward to seeing how each of us will move toward the person God created us to be. His plans for us to utilize the talents He wove in our DNA when He knitted us together in our mothers' wombs."

That concept reawakened her to just how wonderful God was. They had learned through all that happened in the last eleven days that they could trust Him to bring it to pass, like the Scripture in Psalm 37 said.

Malcolm got up and retrieved a large flat box she hadn't noticed before. It was leaning against the wall behind the sofa. "Here's my gift for you today."

She lifted the lid and gasped. "It's your tartan, isn't it?"

"No." He helped her take it from the box. She stood beside him as he stretched it out and gathered it near the middle. He draped it under one of her arms and crossed it so one end went toward the back over her other shoulder and the other end hung in the front. "It's *your* tartan. The brooch I gave you yesterday will hold it right here."

For the first time, she felt they truly were engaged, even if she didn't have a ring. She pulled his head toward hers and initiated a kiss.

"Thank you, Malcolm. I'll take it upstairs. How do I put it back into the box?"

He showed her how to fold it then sent her on her way.

This really is happening. Thank you, Jesus.

AS SHE DRESSED for the carols, communion, and candlelight service, Alanza gazed longingly at the box containing the tartan. She wished she could wear it tonight. But she would have to wait until she was Mrs. Malcolm MacGregor. Woven of the finest wool, the tartan was large enough to use for a blanket if you happened to be caught out in cold weather. She'd have to do some research to learn just how many ways Scots historically used them.

As she put the bow clip in her hair, she marveled that Malcolm's courting gifts started with a tartan-ribbon bow and ended with the real thing. She wondered if he planned it that way. Some of the gifts from him seemed spur of the moment, like the earrings and the roses to make up for the incident with Jessica. He may have planned the first and last gifts, but not the rest. She loved him for himself, but she also enjoyed his thoughtful gifts to her.

She went downstairs to find all of the MacGregor family ready. They were supposed to meet her parents at the east end of the church lobby in about twenty minutes. It took three cars to carry all of them comfortably.

Tonight, Malcolm drove his car. She worried about his injuries. During the last two days, purple bruises appeared on his arms and his right jaw. She was sure there were other bruises that she couldn't see. Her heart melted when she remembered how he threw himself at her assailant, knowing there was a chance he could be hurt or killed by the crazed man swinging

the sharp knife. She thanked God that he hadn't plunged it into one of Malcolm's vital organs. She had to push those thoughts away. *Malcolm is fine. He's sitting right beside me.*

When they arrived at church, Isobel took her two little ones to the nursery, where volunteers had activities for the older children and played with the infants, sang, or read stories to them.

The man who worked security for the laundromat mission was ushering and led everyone else to a space he'd saved for them on one side of the sanctuary, near the front. He remained standing by Malcolm while waiting for the service to start. They carried on quite a conversation from the looks of it. Soon Malcolm came to sit beside her. She'd saved him the spot on her left at the end of the row, so no one would bump his sore arm.

A choir on risers backed up the praise team and Alanza lost herself in the music. Everyone in the sanctuary lifted their voices in carols like groups of angels. She was sure heaven would sound and feel something like this.

When the carol singing ended, ushers passed out the communion bread and grape juice. It took a lot of ushers spread all over the sanctuary to get the elements to everyone in attendance. And they did it without taking very long, even with this large crowd. While the elements were being passed, a soloist offered a moving rendition of "O Holy Night." It gave Alanza goosebumps. Her eyes filled with tears and she wiped them away.

Malcolm pulled her closer under his arm. She felt so peaceful and at home there. The pastor who welcomed them to the supper of the Lamb of God tied the communion to all that Jesus did to connect people with His father. Alanza felt clean and renewed after this portion of the service.

Each person had received a candle when they entered the sanctuary. Now, another pastor spoke about Jesus bringing light

into the world. And all of the church lights were turned off, save the tiny ones on the emergency boxes on the wall. The pastors took candles from the communion table and used them to light the ushers' candles. The ushers then walked through the sanctuary, even into the balcony, to light the worshippers' candles. As each candle was lit, everyone passed the flame to anyone who needed it.

Alanza basked in the radiance as it grew and grew, until the whole sanctuary was filled with bright candlelight. The worship team led the congregation in singing "Silent Night" *a cappella*, before the candles were extinguished.

After the service, the MacGregor and the Cantalamessa families went into the lobby to mingle with both their friends and newcomers.

Malcolm leaned toward her. "The security guard told me the attacker at the laundromat was so high on drugs, it took them a while to figure out what he was saying. He was trying to kidnap you for ransom, to get money for drugs. He'd spent time near Cantalamessa's and knew your family sometimes gave food to the homeless in the area. He saw you and recognized you."

"Really?" She shivered, so thankful again that Malcolm had come to her rescue and the assailant was in jail.

Having overheard part of their conversation, the men from their families gathered around them. Poppa asked Malcolm to repeat what he'd told her.

"Is he still in custody?" Poppa looked grim.

"Yes. He's being charged with kidnapping. It's his third arrest for a serious crime. Even if he tries to make a plea deal, he will automatically be sent to prison without a chance of parole." Malcolm shook his head. "I know that has to happen,

but I'll pray that the prison ministry can reach him and turn him toward the Lord."

He gave Alanza a tight squeeze. "And I'm thankful he didn't hurt Alanza more than he did."

"Hey, Mal." Eric's voice came from close by. He clapped Malcolm on the back.

"So you really meant it when you told me you were coming back to church." Malcolm smiled from ear to ear.

Eric nodded. "I've turned over a new leaf. And you'll never guess who I saw here tonight."

Alanza was curious. "Who?"

Eric turned to her and grinned. "You must be Alanza. I'm Eric." She smiled back and they shook hands. "Mal told me about what happened at the restaurant last week with Jessica. And that he suggested she try going to church."

Malcolm put his arm around Alanza's waist. "So she decided to come tonight?"

"Yeah, but she came on Sunday first. She didn't know this is where you go to church. And me, too, now. She met up with people in the singles ministry and she's making friends. And she looks like her old self, not like the Jez she was calling herself."

"Wow." Alanza smiled up at Malcolm. "I'm so glad we've been praying for her."

21

Wednesday – Christmas Day

Alanza went home with her parents last night after the service and the wonderful feast at the MacGregor home. So they would have their special family breakfast on Christmas morning: waffles with strawberries and whipped cream on top. Mamma only made them on special occasions like Christmas.

They exchanged presents after breakfast. Alanza thought about her brothers, missing them like crazy. She hoped they would get a chance to call today.

As they were unwrapping their gifts, the phone rang. Poppa picked it up. "Hello… Don? Where are you now?"

She and Mamma gathered around him, so he put the call on speaker. "Hi, yes, it's Don. Tony is right here beside me. I'm using the speaker on this call, so we can both hear you. We're

in Kuwait right now and an American phone company has this room set up, so we can call home for free."

Both women squealed with excitement when they heard the twin brothers were stationed together now.

"This is Tony. Is that Mamma and Alanza?"

"Who else?" Poppa laughed. "You know how excitable the women in this family are. Are both of you all right?"

"Yes, Poppa. God has been protecting us." Donatello's voice brought calm with it. "Oh, we have occasional bumps and scrapes but nothing more."

Alanza jumped into the conversation. "Are both of you still coming home early in January? Can you stay until January 18?"

"What happens on January 18?"

"My wedding."

Her brothers started hollering and talking at the same time when they realized what she said. Alanza and their parents couldn't understand a single word.

Poppa said, "My *polpetti*! Please take turns speaking, we can't understand you." He sat down at the table.

"Why are we just now finding out about a wedding?" Tony's voice came through loud and clear. "I haven't even heard about a boyfriend."

Alanza laughed. "It's a recent development."

"How recent?" Don's voice sounded sharp.

"Almost two weeks."

"Poppa? Mamma? Are you okay with this?" Tony didn't sound happy either.

The Cantalamessas looked at each other and Jacolin nodded to her husband. "Donatello, Donatino, your Mamma and I appreciate your concern for your sister. We really do. We

weren't okay with the idea at first, but we're very pleased with the young man who has been courting her."

"Is that what he's calling it? Courting?" Don sounded as if he wished he were in the room with them. "What dude in this day and age uses words like that?"

"Don, Tony, it's all right. He asked my permission to date Alanza before he even asked her out. He respects me... and your sister."

"We'll withhold our opinion until we get to meet him," Tony huffed.

Mamma's sweet voice chimed in. "You'll like him."

The conversation turned to other subjects and continued for almost half an hour before the twins had to hang up.

Now Christmas felt complete.

ALANZA RODE WITH her parents as they headed toward the MacGregor home. She really looked forward to spending her first Christmas with her soon-to-be in-laws.

When they arrived, Poppa parked in the circular driveway and they went to the front door. Immediately, Malcolm opened it and welcomed them in. Wonderful smells filled the air and Alanza's stomach growled. Maybe she should have had more waffles.

Soon, everyone was seated at the long table in the formal dining room, with the little ones in high chairs.

Every kind of holiday fare was available, especially gourmet dishes. Way too many choices for Alanza to try them all. Every bite she put in her mouth was delicious. She had a hard time stopping when she was full. There were so many other foods she hadn't tried. *Maybe another time.*

Angus and his baby sister were the center of attention for much of the meal. When Isobel wanted to take them to another room, her father smiled at her.

"They are our next generation and they need to be included in family gatherings. I can hold Kirsty so you can eat." Maxwell came around the table and gathered his granddaughter in his arms.

When he sat down, he started feeding her little morsels from his plate. She grinned and giggled with every bite.

Alanza was glad he would be her children's grandfather.

When everyone finished, Maxwell suggested they all go into the parlor, where dessert would be served.

Bella stopped Alanza to talk to her about the wedding, while everyone else got settled in the den. When they arrived, there were only two empty seats and Malcolm was nowhere to be found. Bella sat in one chair, so Alanza took the other. Conversations resumed all around the room.

No one sat close enough for Alanza to talk to anyone. She looked for somewhere she could perch so she could join in a conversation—a footstool or even the hearth—but there were no free spots. She began to feel excluded.

All at once, everyone stopped talking. She looked toward the foyer.

There was Malcolm, in full Scottish regalia. Knee-length socks with tartan plaid at the tops. Shoes she'd never seen before with some kind of lacing up his legs. A kilt in MacGregor tartan plaid, a purse-like pouch hanging in front. A snowy white shirt, black vest, and fitted black jacket. A black, brimless hat. A fine figure of a man. Her heart beat furiously and she had a hard time catching her breath. *Mamma mia! Just. Wow.*

She forced herself to look away and saw that every single eye in the room was trained on her. Apparently, everyone else knew what was going on—everyone, that is, except her parents, who looked as confused as she felt.

Over the drumming of her accelerated heartbeat, Alanza imagined she could hear bagpipes playing a lilting melody, almost like a love song. Then she realized there *was* bagpipe music coming closer to the parlor.

With a regal bearing, Malcolm walked toward her. Was that why no one was sitting nearby? They all knew what he was doing? *Of course, they do.* And that's why Bella stopped to talk to her. To delay her. To make sure she took the seat she did.

In one swift, graceful movement, Malcolm knelt on one knee in front of her. *Are little Scottish boys taught how to move with such elegance wearing kilts?* She covered her mouth with one hand.

"Alanza, I've loved you since I first laid eyes on you. You captured my heart and I believe God created us for each other. I would be most blessed if you would accept me to be your husband." He bowed his head as if he were whispering a prayer… and maybe he was. Somewhere nearby, the bagpipes continued to play.

When he raised his head, his Texas-sky-blue eyes stared straight into hers. "I love you with all my heart, Alanza. Would you consent to be my wife?"

She was so overcome with emotion that words would not leave her throat. And she couldn't look away from his mesmerizing gaze. She didn't notice he was holding a small open jewelry box until Bella spoke. "Alanza, look in his hand."

Glancing down, she saw a stunning gold ring. A large ruby was the centerpiece, with pearls ringing it, and smaller emeralds surrounded them in a gold setting. The colors of the MacGregor tartan.

"Yes," she whispered. Her left hand shook as she held it out for Malcolm. "Oh, yes."

He slipped the ring on her finger. It fit perfectly. *Of course, he wouldn't leave anything to chance! He found out my ring size.* He stood and held out his hand to raise her up beside him, then he took her into his arms and kissed her until her legs almost gave way beneath her.

Well, I got my proposal. And it was worth waiting for.

When their kiss ended, still in each other's arms, Alanza noticed the bagpiper standing in the doorway, dressed in a clan outfit similar to Malcolm's.

"Who's that?" she whispered. "And what is he playing?"

"That's my Uncle Seamus. The song is 'For the Love of a Princess.'"

Her eyes sparkled, filled with joyful tears. "Do you think he would play the bagpipes for our wedding?"

Malcolm smiled down at her. "Anything for you, Princess Alanza."

Then so much joy filled her heart that she started to laugh. Soon Malcolm joined in. And as the song ended, everyone

cheered and applauded as they rushed up to congratulate the happy couple.

EPILOGUE

August 1

Alanza stared down at DFW Airport just before the corporate jet started circling, preparing to descend toward one of the runways. "I'm glad to be home, Mal, aren't you?" She turned to look at her husband of six months.

He was looking at her instead of the ever-nearer ground. "Home is anywhere I'm with you."

"I know, but I've missed the good old USA, haven't you?"

Malcolm smiled and leaned his head back against the seat. "I've loved every minute we were in Australia. Look at how much each of us has grown spiritually. But I *have* missed seeing our families whenever we want to."

"I'm glad they came to Australia to visit. I didn't think Poppa and Mamma would ever travel that far. But they did come and

had a really good time." She laughed. "I'll never forget Poppa and that kangaroo!"

The pilot's voice came over the intercom. "Folks, we have just been cleared to land at Dallas/Fort Worth International Airport. Please check to make sure your seat belt is securely fastened for our approach."

Alanza shifted in her seat and complied. "I wonder who will meet us at the airport."

When the plane came to a full stop, they unbuckled and headed toward the exit. "Thank you for taking such good care of us," Alanza told the flight attendant.

The woman smiled at her. "You're welcome. My pleasure."

Alanza stepped through the door, stood on the top step, and glanced around.

"Where are we? I've never been to this part of the airport."

Malcolm stood behind her. "This is where corporate jets land."

They started walking down the steps side by side with Malcolm holding her hand. "They'll unload all our things from the plane and have it delivered to *Faither*'s house. We'll sort things out there."

A stretch limo drove toward them on the tarmac. It arrived just when they reached the bottom step. The doors opened and Maxwell, Bella, Alessandro, and Jacolin got out.

Alanza ran toward her parents and hugged them both at the same time. The hot summer wind blew her cotton dress against her belly.

Jacolin grinned happily at Alessandro. "Poppa, I hope you're ready to be a grandfather."

He looked at Alanza. "You weren't expecting when we were in Australia, were you?"

"Poppa, you came for a visit just two months after we got there. I'm only a little over three months along." Mamma hugged her again as Malcolm and his family joined them.

"Did you hear that?" Jacolin smiled at Maxwell. "We're going to be grandparents!"

"That's terrific!" He beamed at Alanza.

Bella came over. "So tell me all about what you did in Australia while Mal was slaving away. Daddy isn't very talkative. He didn't tell me much."

Alanza reached for Malcolm's hand as he came beside her. "We went sightseeing when Malcolm had time off. Being in Brisbane, we were near the Great Barrier Reef, the rain forests, and the Gold Coast. We even visited Sydney once. I've always wanted to see the Opera House. And before we left Texas, Mal told me that since I wouldn't be working, he wanted me to pursue my dreams. So that's what I did. I've been painting. Even won a blue ribbon at an art show. I've wanted to write a novel and I was able to connect with other Christian authors, who encouraged me. And I just received a contract from an agent here in the U.S. to represent my first book."

Everyone greeted this news with woots and more hugs.

Malcolm put his arm around Alanza's waist. "I'm very proud of her."

She put her own arm around him. "And I'm so proud to have you as my husband and father to our child…" She patted her baby bump. "…the most precious gift you've given me."

ALANZA'S
BEST HOT CHOCOLATE

Ingredients

4 cups milk

1/2 cup sugar

1/3 cup good quality cocoa powder

3 tbls. honey

1 tsp. vanilla extract

1 dark chocolate bar

1 can real whipped cream

Maraschino cherries

Instructions

Heat milk over medium to low heat, stirring constantly until milk starts to bubble slightly (about 10 minutes). Meanwhile, mix sugar and cocoa together until well blended. When milk is ready, gradually add in sugar, cocoa, and honey, stirring constantly. Put heat on low and add shavings of chocolate bar and vanilla. Continue stirring until chocolate has melted. Remove from heat and pour into mugs. Add whipped cream, chocolate shavings, and cherries on top, as desired.

ABOUT THE AUTHOR

*A*ward-winning author Lena Nelson Dooley has written more than forty books, which have sold more than 900,000 copies. Her books have appeared on the bestseller lists of the Christian Booksellers Association, the Evangelical Christian Publishers Association, and *Publisher's Weekly*, as well as some Amazon bestseller lists. She is a member of American Christian Fiction Writers, its local chapter, ACFW-DFW, the Christian Authors' Network, and Gateway Church in Southlake, Texas. She also writes a popular blog that features other authors' books.

Lena is a three-time finalist in the Carol Awards ACFW contest. Her 2010 release, *Love Finds You in Golden, New Mexico*, won the 2011 Will Rogers Medallion Award for excellence in publishing Western Fiction. Her next series, McKenna's

Daughters: Maggie's Journey appeared on a reviewers' Top Ten Books of 2011 list. It also won the 2012 Selah award for Historical Novel. The second, Mary's Blessing, was a Selah Award finalist for Romance novel. Catherine's Pursuit, released in 2013, was the winner of the NTRWA Carolyn Reader's Choice contest, took second place in the CAN Golden Scroll Novel of the Year award, and won the Will Rogers Medallion bronze medallion. Her book, A Heart's Gift, won RWA's Faith, Hope, and Love Readers' Choice Award in July 2017. Her blog, A Christian Writer's World, received the Readers' Choice Blog of the Year Award from the Book Club Network.

Lena also has experience in screenwriting, acting, directing, and voice-overs, and currently serves on the board of directors of Higher Ground Films. She has been featured in articles in Christian Fiction Online Magazine, ACFW Journal, Book Fun Magazine, Charisma Magazine, and Christian Retailing.

In addition to her writing, Lena is a frequent speaker at women's groups, writers' groups, and regional and national conferences. She is the host of The Lena Nelson Dooley Show on the Along Came a Writer blogtalk radio network. Lena has an active web presence on Facebook, Twitter, Goodreads, and Linkedin, as well as her internationally connected blog, where she interviews other authors and promotes their books.

FIND THE
AUTHOR ONLINE

Website: www.lenanelsondooley.com

Blog: http://lenanelsondooley.blogspot.com

Pinterest: http://pinterest.com/lenandooley/

Facebook: www.facebook.com/lena.nelson.dooley

Official fan page: www.facebook.com/pages/
Lena-Nelson-Dooley/42960748768?ref=ts

Twitter: www.twitter.com/lenandooley

Goodreads: http://www.goodreads.com/author/show/333031.
Lena_Nelson_Dooley

Blogtalk Radio: http://www.blogtalkradio.com/search/
along-came-a-writer/

Instagram: www.instagram.com/lenanelsondooley

Amazon author page: http://www.amazon.com/-/e/
B001JPAIDE

LinkedIn: https://www.linkedin.com/in/lenanelsondooley

Welcome to Our House!

We Have a Special Gift for You ...

It is our privilege and pleasure to share in your love of Christian fiction by publishing books that enrich your life and encourage your faith.

To show our appreciation, we invite you to sign up to receive a specially selected **Reader Appreciation Gift**, with our compliments. Just go to the Web address at the bottom of this page.

God bless you as you seek a deeper walk with Him!

WE HAVE A GIFT FOR YOU. VISIT:

whpub.me/fictionthx

WHITAKER
HOUSE